MW01147217

IDA B. WELLS

❧ Also by ❧

ERICA ARMSTRONG DUNBAR
and CANDACE BUFORD

Susie King Taylor

RISE. RISK. REMEMBER.
INCREDIBLE STORIES OF COURAGEOUS BLACK WOMEN

IDA B. WELLS
Journalist, Advocate & Crusader for Justice

Erica Armstrong Dunbar
& Candace Buford

Aladdin

New York   Amsterdam/Antwerp   London
Toronto   Sydney/Melbourne   New Delhi

If you purchased this book without a cover, you should be aware that this book is stolen property. It was reported as "unsold and destroyed" to the publisher, and neither the author nor the publisher has received any payment for this "stripped book."

ALADDIN

An imprint of Simon & Schuster Children's Publishing Division
1230 Avenue of the Americas, New York, New York 10020
For more than 100 years, Simon & Schuster has championed authors and the stories they create. By respecting the copyright of an author's intellectual property, you enable Simon & Schuster and the author to continue publishing exceptional books for years to come. We thank you for supporting the author's copyright by purchasing an authorized edition of this book.
No amount of this book may be reproduced or stored in any format, nor may it be uploaded to any website, database, language-learning model, or other repository, retrieval, or artificial intelligence system without express permission. All rights reserved. Inquiries may be directed to Simon & Schuster, 1230 Avenue of the Americas, New York, NY 10020 or permissions@simonandschuster.com.
First Aladdin paperback edition June 2025
Text copyright © 2025 by Erica Armstrong Dunbar
Cover illustration copyright © 2025 by Lisbeth Checo
Southern Horrors: Lynch Law in All its Phases by Ida B. Wells-Barnett was originally published as a pamphlet in 1892.
Also available in an Aladdin hardcover edition.
All rights reserved, including the right of reproduction in whole or in part in any form.
ALADDIN and related logo are registered trademarks of Simon & Schuster, LLC.
For information about special discounts for bulk purchases, please contact Simon & Schuster Special Sales at 1-866-506-1949 or business@simonandschuster.com.
The Simon & Schuster Speakers Bureau can bring authors to your live event.
For more information or to book an event contact the Simon & Schuster Speakers Bureau at 1-866-248-3049 or visit our website at www.simonspeakers.com.
Cover design by Karin Paprocki | Interior design by Mike Rosamilia
The text of this book was set in Perpetua.
Manufactured in the United States of America 0425 BID
2 4 6 8 10 9 7 5 3 1
Library of Congress Cataloging-in-Publication Data
Names: Dunbar, Erica Armstrong, author. | Buford, Candace, author.
Title: Ida B. Wells / by Erica Armstrong Dunbar and Candace Buford.
Description: First Aladdin paperback edition. | New York, New York : Aladdin, 2025. | Series: Rise. Risk. Remember. Incredible Stories of Courageous Black Women | Summary: "Meet journalist and activist Ida B. Wells in this second vibrant middle grade biography in the Rise. Risk. Remember. Incredible Stories series spotlighting Black women who left their mark on history from acclaimed and New York Times bestselling author Erica Armstrong Dunbar and Candace Buford. Born into slavery, Ida B. Wells (1862-1931) grew up watching her family fight for Black rights during the Reconstruction Era. After receiving her education, Ida worked as an educator before moving to Memphis where she began writing about white mob violence, investigating lynchings and reporting her findings in local newspapers. Ida helped found the NAACP and was a renowned leader in the civil rights movement, but she was also a young woman desperately trying to hold her family together after tragedy with dignity and resolve. Ida fought to give voice to the people suffering from injustice, racism, and violence. She spoke out against lynchings internationally and refused to cater to the white women leading the suffrage movement. Throughout her life, she devoted her words and deeds to activism"—Provided by publisher.
Identifiers: LCCN 2024052142 (print) | LCCN 2024052143 (ebook) |
ISBN 9781665919838 (hardcover) | ISBN 9781665919821 (paperback) | ISBN 9781665919845 (ebook)
Subjects: LCSH: Wells-Barnett, Ida B., 1862-1931—Juvenile literature. | African American women civil rights workers—Biography—Juvenile literature. | Civil rights workers—United States—Biography—Juvenile literature. | African American women educators—Biography—Juvenile literature. | African American women journalists—Biography—Juvenile literature. | United States—Race relations—Juvenile literature. | African Americans—Civil rights—History—Juvenile literature. | African Americans—Social conditions—To 1964—Juvenile literature.
Classification: LCC E185.97.W55 D86 2025 (print) | LCC E185.97.W55 (ebook) | DDC 323.092 [B]—dc23/eng/20241129
LC record available at https://lccn.loc.gov/2024052142

We dedicate this book to the journalists who shed light on our country's darkest truths.

—E. A. D. and C. B.

Authors' Note

Welcome, readers!

We are happy to introduce you to our second biography of an incredible and courageous Black woman. Ida Bell Wells-Barnett is known by many as a journalist, activist, and crusader for justice, and we are honored to include her life story in our series. Much is known about Ida B. Wells-Barnett, in part because she kept diaries, wrote articles, pamphlets, and letters, and was the center of attention in many circles. She was written about often (sometimes in a positive light and sometimes in a negative one) and she left behind some of the most powerful political writing of her era. For that we are grateful.

Ida Bell Wells was born enslaved in Holly Springs, Mississippi, on July 16, 1862. Technically, Ida and her parents were free after the Emancipation Proclamation was issued on January 1, 1863, but the Wells family wouldn't truly know or experience freedom until the Civil War ended. She was raised by loving parents whose lives were cut short by a yellow fever epidemic. At the age of sixteen, Ida chose to pause her own dreams and take care of her siblings. She began a teaching career that allowed her to feed her family.

We decided to focus this book on the earlier years of Ida's life. We are fascinated by the way that Ida was able to do so very much at such a young age. Like with our other books in this series, we made the decision to write this from a first-person point of view, a choice that allows us to use "informed speculation" about her feelings and that allows us to draw readers in to her dramatic life. Wherever possible, we draw on Ida's own words and we have included one of the most powerful primary sources written by any Black journalist of her era. *Southern Horrors: Lynch Law in All Its Phases* was published in 1892. Ida wrote this powerful pamphlet following the murder of her friend Tommie Moss in Memphis, Tennessee. Moss and many other Black men and women were the victims of lynching, a form of violence that threatened Black people for nearly a century. Ida wrote courageously about this form of violence and exposed the evil behind it, even when this kind of writing put her own life in harm's way.

Once again, we made the decision to use words that are more contemporary, such as "Black" and "enslaved," in order to dignify Ida, her family, and the millions of Black men and women who endured bondage and the afterlife of slavery.

Ida B. Wells-Barnett's crusade for justice is a reminder of the power of the written word. We encourage you all to read her story and to continue the tradition of speaking and writing your truth.

—Erica Armstrong Dunbar &
Candace Buford

Chapter 1

WHEN MY FATHER CAME HOME FROM work, he smelled of sandpaper and sawdust, of earthy notes mixed with wood stains and sweat. His carpenter's hands were calloused but not as rough as some of the other men.

He had started working for his enslaver, who was also his father. When he was old enough, he was brought here, to Holly Springs, Mississippi, to apprentice his carpenter trade. When the war ended, my father snatched his freedom.

One of the beautiful moments from my father's time in Marshall County, Mississippi, was meeting my mother. He married her while they were both still enslaved. And then married her again when they both had their freedom.

By the way his eyes twinkled when he looked at her, I figured he'd marry her over and over again.

He opened his arms and wrapped them around Mama.

"Come here and let me give you a squeeze."

"Oh hush." Mama blushed, swatting him away. By the way she clamped down on her lips, though, I could tell she was amused. She turned back to her cooking, pots bubbling on the stove, and said over her shoulder, "Supper isn't ready yet, but will be soon."

"That's all right. I walked back with some of the other Masons to discuss the news. We'll sit outside for a while yet."

"Can I come too?" I asked. "Please? I finished all my schoolwork. Please?"

"Listen to that child!" My mother chuckled by the stove. She looked over at me. "Just as persistent as the day she was born."

Mama said I popped into the world with urgency, which seemed right. As much as I enjoyed attending school, I loved listening to my father talk politics with the leading men of our community. The sun was setting on my childhood—at sixteen years old, I was on the cusp of womanhood. And I had as much interest in America's Reconstruction as any man. This was a time of rapid change, a reintegration of the Confederate states into the Union and an establishing of equal rights for emancipated Black people.

I folded my arms, waiting for permission.

"Oh, all right, fine." Mama sighed and then turned back to her bubbling pot.

I followed closely behind my father as he walked to the porch. My sister Eugenia, who was sitting next to the fireplace, shrugged her shoulders at me. I returned her indifference with an eye roll. She didn't understand why I bothered with politics instead of choosing to play with my friends. In fact, none of my siblings showed much interest in the news of the day. But I found it all very fascinating and important. I was almost an adult, and I felt an urgency that things were changing. I just wasn't sure they were changing for the better.

But I wanted to be at the center of it all.

My father reclined in his chair on the porch, surrounded by some of his friends, many of whom were also involved in the community. They were tired from working all day but still wanted to gather to talk about the things that were changing. The chapter of Radical Reconstruction, which had ushered in a whole bunch of Black politicians, congressmen, and even two senators across the South, promised hope and optimism in the days following the Civil War. With slavery ended, these Republican statesmen tried to construct laws that would protect the rights of formerly enslaved people and Black people across the country. But the rift between Democrats and Republicans remained as wide as the Mississippi River, and the new legal protections for Black Americans were already being chipped away. It was 1878 and only thirteen years had passed since the end of the Civil War, but it felt like things were moving backward. I could see the worry on my father's face as he shifted in his chair. I sat on the porch near his feet, ready to hang on his every word.

"Why don't you read tonight, Ida," he said as he unfurled his newspaper from his breast pocket and handed it to me.

"Yes, sir." I reached for the paper. I couldn't help the smile that tugged at my lips. Children weren't usually permitted to be part of adult conversations, especially female children. But I happily jumped at the chance.

So I sat on my perch in front of these men and read the news of the day to my father and his friends. Although they were all skilled tradesmen and community leaders, some of them did not know how to read. Their weary spirits seemed revived as I confidently read out loud. My father's eyes were alert. He was enlivened. His friends leaned forward, nodding me on in encouragement, maybe even admiration.

But flipping the page to read the next headline, I stumbled over the words. I took a breath and read on.

INNOCENT BLOOD SHED
The two events of the past fortnight, which the Recording angel of God put down to the debt of this country, were the lynching of a colored woman in Virginia, charged with inciting a boy to burn a barn, and the hanging of two colored men in Delaware believed by nine out of every ten to be innocent.

I paused, letting the words sink in. Three people had been lynched—*murdered* without a trial. I shifted uncomfortably, thinking about how frightened I was. There were laws meant to protect people from being condemned without a trial. But those laws did not seem to extend to Black people, not even innocent ones.

"Let me see that," my father mumbled under his breath as he slid the paper from my hands. His eyes scanned the page and he tightened his lips in a scowl. He glanced at the surrounding men. "It was probably the Klan."

I'd heard the name of this group before. Whoever they were, this KKK group had all the men looking tense. I heard my mother and father talk about them and knew they were the reason for the anxious way my mother walked the floor at night when my father was out at a political meeting. Yet as far as I knew, the Klan hadn't burned down anything in Holly Springs.

The floorboards creaked behind the front door, and I could tell that my mother was inside pacing now. She worried when my father was out at political meetings, but when he managed to have them here, she was doubly nervous there would be some retribution.

"They aren't *claiming* responsibility." My father rolled his eyes with a tight smile.

"They didn't say they didn't do it neither," said a younger gentleman named Timothy from his seat on the porch railing.

"So the Klan is stirring up trouble again. How long you think we have until they come to Holly Springs, Jim?" The man looked at my father, his wide eyes filled with fear.

"These men will come *here*?" I gulped, grabbing my father's leg.

"It's okay." My father grazed my cheek with the backs of his fingers. His face was tight with worry, but he looked into my eyes. He didn't fool me, but I found comfort in his efforts. He shook his head slightly and said, softly, "I won't let them get anywhere near you."

The front door swung open and my mother appeared, her anxious eyebrows upturned. She was slightly flushed, probably from all the pacing she was doing.

"Come here, child." My mother snapped her fingers at me. She pursed her lips in a tight line and cocked her head to the side, waiting. "Well, come on then."

"Listen to your mama," my father said as he nodded his head. When he turned to look at my mother's arched eyebrows, he sighed, his shoulders deflating. "She has to learn the truth somehow."

"I don't want the Klan mentioned in this house," my mother said. She stomped her foot on the threshold, emphasizing her claim on her own front door. "They're already in the streets. I won't have them casting shadows on this house and giving my babies nightmares."

"But——" I started to say that I wanted to hear more about it. My father was right: I had to learn the truth. But my mother raised a menacing eyebrow, one that meant for me to do as I was told. My time on the porch had come to a swift and decisive end.

"Why don't you all get washed up for supper," my grandmother said, leaning around my mother in the doorway. She didn't live here. But when she spoke, my daddy listened.

"All right, Mama, we're finishing up here in a moment's time."

As the door shut behind me, I could hear the conversation continue, a little quieter than before, with hushed whispers of politics that my father didn't want us to overhear. Of course, I had already overheard things around town on my way to school. My parents couldn't shield me from the world forever.

When I came inside, I was met with the boisterous noise that often filled our house. We were a large brood, the Wells family. I had three younger sisters and three younger brothers, and we were never short of liveliness. Eugenia, Annie, Lily, James, George, baby Stanley, and I kept my parents busy.

Eugenia, who was the closest in age to me, sat in her chair near the fire. Her legs, which had stopped working when she was younger, were covered in a blanket. She waved me over to join her.

"I was supposed to wash up for dinner and help Mother," I said, eyeing the long kitchen table where my brothers were fighting over a wooden toy and my sisters were engaged in a fit of laughter.

"I think there's enough going on there," Genie, the nickname I called Eugenia, said as she smiled mischievously and slid a book from underneath her blanket. She passed it to me. "I just finished reading this. It's good."

"Oh, *Little Women*!" My fingers grazed over the hardcover,

itching to crack it open and begin reading. But Mama plucked the book away from me before I could even read the title page.

"Come on, girls. You know you're only supposed to read the Bible on Sundays."

"But I've already read the Bible through once. Plus, Father let me read from the newspaper tonight," I whined. I looked longingly at the book that was now firmly locked in my mother's grasp. She raised an eyebrow, a challenge for me to keep mouthing off to her. I sighed and said, "Yes, ma'am."

"Here you go." Eugenia reached under her chair and quickly produced a Bible.

"What else you got under there?" I asked, smirking as I studied her armchair. She broke out into a toothy grin and I joined her. My sister, who was limited in her mobility, was always ahead of everyone with her mischievous nature.

"I'll put this in your bag," Mother said as she walked over to my suitcase. "You can read it on your trip to Grandma's house."

"Mama, I already have enough books to finish my homework."

"Good. You can read any chance you get." She looked over her shoulder as the bag flapped shut. "Your job isn't just learning in school. It's taking every opportunity to enrich your mind. Understood?"

"Yes, ma'am." Just then my nostrils puckered up at the smell coming from the stove. "Are those pork chops?"

"And buttermilk biscuits." Mama wagged her head from

side to side, evidently pleased with herself. "Mr. Boling has been trying to get my recipe for years. Had to politely let him down again today. It was my mama's secret, and it's all I have left of her."

She shrugged and turned back to the stove, hiding her unshed tears. After the war, Mama had tried to find her family in Virginia, but she never saw them again. She and her two sisters were sold as slaves, but fortunately they all lived in Mississippi, not too far from one another. My mother loved her sisters. This was made clear when my mother gave me the middle name Bell in honor of her sister Belle. For my mother, her husband, children, and sisters were her top priority.

"What's the secret to the biscuits?" I asked, leaning toward the kitchen to get another whiff of them.

"If I didn't give it up for my employer, what makes you think I'd tell you?" my mother asked playfully. She laughed when I shrugged sheepishly. "I'll tell you when you're older."

Mama was known far and wide for her cooking, and she still worked for Mr. Boling.

"I suspect Boling is still mad that Jim didn't stay on and work with him after he was apprenticed," Grandma said. "When my son makes up his mind, there's no turning him around."

"He would have gladly stayed on," my mother said. "But after he refused to vote Democrat the way the old man wanted him to, Jim turned up and the shop was locked. Jim had to go find work for himself."

"I suppose it was for the best." Grandma waved her hand

dismissively. She sank into the kitchen chair with a sigh and turned to me with a smile. "All your friends are so excited to see you when you come to Tippah County with me." Then she looked over at the window, listening to my father's muffled voice on the porch, almost like she was making sure he wasn't within earshot. "And Miss Polly would probably love to see you once you get settled in."

"Miss Polly?" My mother's ice-cold voice came from the edge of the stove. Her eyes narrowed to slits. "You taking my daughter to the plantation?"

I looked from mother to my grandmother, shrinking back to the wall so that I wouldn't be in the cross fire. Mama was shooting daggers with her stern scowl. The front door creaked open, drawing everyone's attention to that side of the house, where my father was stepping over the threshold.

"All right, y'all. I'll see you around tomorrow." He waved goodbye to his friends and closed the door behind him. When he looked to the rest of us, he frowned at the silent stiffness emanating from the kitchen. "Uh-oh. What'd I step in?"

"Your mother," my mother said, whipping her dishcloth over her shoulder then planting her hands on her hips. "Your mother wants to take our daughter to see Miss Polly when she's over in Tippah County. To the old man's plantation house."

"Oh." My father nodded and stepped carefully toward my mother. His smile slowly melted into a scowl that mirrored my mother's.

I didn't remember being in bondage. Born in Holly Springs, Mississippi, in the summer of 1862, I was emancipated before I could scarcely walk. But my parents remembered it. The scars of enslavement were much deeper in their memories, though they tried to put it behind them.

My grandmother, who still lived near the old plantation, was still steeped in that old world. She cleared her throat, speaking softly. "As you know, I've been taking care of Miss Polly in her old age. I talk about you and the children most every day." She hesitated, chewing on the inside of her cheek. "She'd love to see you too—if you just come home for a few days, I'm sure I can have it all arranged."

"No, Mother. Not this again."

"I just think . . ." Grandmother started, but my father cut her off.

"I know you've forgiven her. I don't know how you've forgiven her—only by God's good grace, I suppose. But I haven't." My father's frown hardened when he spoke about Miss Polly. Miss Polly was married to his biological father. They had been the enslavers of the plantation. He turned away from my grandmother so that she wouldn't feel the full brunt of his ire. "I'll never forget how she had you whipped. When the old man died, she had them rip your dress so that you could feel the lash on your skin. I'll never forget that."

Grandma bowed her head, her fingers fidgeting in her lap. "She is sorry for it."

"Oh, she apologized for it?" My father raised a skeptical eyebrow.

"Well, no. But she's shown it in her own way. And now all she wants is companionship. And given that she and her husband never had any children of their own, she is eager to see you, to know how you're faring."

"I think I can safely speak for my wife and me on this. We do not want our daughter—or any of our children—to ever step foot in that house."

"Agreed." Mama nodded definitively, jutting her chin out. "We don't want anything to do with that woman. I've felt the whip many times. Enough times to know that a slaver's heart is hardened. And I don't want to expose my children to that. My Ida may have been born enslaved, but the rest of her life will be lived beyond the gates of any plantation."

"My thoughts exactly," said my father as he straightened his collar and pulled out the kitchen chair at the head of the table. He slumped into his seat, looking weary as he gazed at his mother. "Maybe we should postpone Ida's trip. Just to make sure we understand each other."

"I understand," I said from my silent corner of the room.

Three pairs of eyes turned to focus on me, as if they were surprised to see me there. Children were supposed to be seen but not heard. It was brazen of me to insert myself into grown folks' business. I was still only sixteen—not old enough for a seat at a table or to run my own household. I treaded carefully in this space. "I promise not to go to the plantation."

I clasped my hands as if in prayer, willing my parents to allow me to go. I hadn't been to Grandma's house in ages, and as my grandmother had said, I had some friends there who I wanted to see. And I did like to travel. Tippah County, Mississippi, was only about fifty miles away. I loved to watch the fields change. I loved passing through small towns, looking at all the people I didn't know, wondering what stories they had to tell. I found it all very fascinating.

"All right then, Miss Ida." My father chuckled under his breath. He looked at me for a moment, taking me in. "Seems like you've found your voice. Don't ever lose it."

"I won't." I shook my head, making my pigtails swish across the back of my dress. "Promise."

"And when you get back," my mother said as she gripped my shoulders, bending down to whisper in my ear, "I'll tell you the secret to those biscuits."

And then she kissed me on top of my head.

Chapter 2

A FEW DAYS LATER, I WAS SETTLED INTO MY grandmother's house in Tippah County. It felt like a world apart from that of Holly Springs, which was larger than any town Tippah had to offer. My grandmother, her husband, my uncle, and my aunt worked the land, tilling the soil every season and planting corn and cotton and whatever else would fetch a decent price at market.

I helped with bringing in the crop, saw a few of my friends, and as I promised my mother, I did all of my homework. And in the spaces in between I read. The fields near the house were lush with blooming cotton. The scent filled the air, and I breathed it in as I filled my head with stories. I loved being at my grandmother's house.

But any time my grandmother went into town, I jumped

at the opportunity to do so. As promised, there was no more talk about Miss Polly. My grandmother and I gave the plantation house a wide berth as we walked to town, and I kept close to my grandmother as we walked down the road to the post office. She tutted under her breath as she walked, likely piqued by her latest trip to care for the ailing Miss Polly.

"How was your visit with Mabel?" she asked.

"It was good. She wants to move to Holly Springs so that she can attend Shaw University with me."

"Does she now?" Grandmother yawned, revealing her dwindling interest. She had been in the fields most of the day, and the sun had sizzled away most of her energy.

"She said that the Freedmen's Aid folks aren't planning to build a school here anytime soon." I shrugged, skipping over a rock in the road. "I told her to come on over. Holly Springs opens its doors to everyone. That's what my father says."

"It is growing quickly, especially the colored populations. Which is good. It keeps us safe to be cushioned in our own kind." Grandma folded her arms, her eyes darting to the numerous white folks walking down the street.

We were careful in this part of town. My grandmother never quite looked at white people in the eyes—that was inviting trouble. She kept her head down, and following her, I did the same. Still, I couldn't help but sneak glances into the shop windows, admiring the hats and dresses for sale. And the people milling about were interesting, even if I didn't know their stories.

Everyone had a story.

"Here we are." Grandma reached her hand out to grab the door handle, opening the door for me. She took a deep breath and then followed me into the post office.

It was a simple, small space, much smaller than the one in my hometown. There was only a small desk in the middle of the store with a few odd bits of paper on it. Behind it were rows of wooden cubbies, some stuffed with mail. Most were barren. I imagined this town growing in a similar fashion to Holly Springs. Soon maybe all the mail slots would be filled.

The man sitting at the desk looked up from his notepad long enough to glance quickly at me and my grandmother. His gaze quickly fell back to his desk. "Somethin' you need?"

"Afternoon, sir." My grandmother's voice ticked up a few octaves as she tried to sound as light and pleasant as possible. This man did not deserve that much deference as he was being short with my grandmother.

"I'm here to pick up my mail," my grandmother said.

"Wait over there." He flicked his head to the front corner of the room and finished writing in his notebook, evidently in no hurry to assist us.

The shop bell above the door rang. In stepped a woman in modest clothing—more modest than the dresses my grandmother and I had on. But she was white. The postman looked up from his ledger.

"Good afternoon, Mrs. Percy." His demeanor completely

changed. His mouth widened into a welcoming smile as he closed his book. "How may I be of service?"

While they busied themselves with Mrs. Percy's packages, I talked to Grandmother to pass the time. We whispered to ourselves, not wanting to be overheard. The postman cleared his throat, bringing our attention back toward him.

"Don't dawdle over there," he grumbled under his breath. "Name?"

"Peggy Cheers," Grandmother said as she stepped up to the counter. She blinked quickly, mumbling a correction. "Peggy Cheers, *sir*."

He rummaged in the shelves behind him and grabbed a couple of envelopes. He tossed them on the counter. He pointed to the corner of the table, as if he didn't want to be anywhere near Grandmother's touch. Then he opened his big ledger book and busied himself with ignoring us again.

That's how most white people acted. They wanted to pretend we didn't exist.

We exited quietly and quickly, breathing in the fresh air and flushing out the frustrating stuffiness of the shop. But it wasn't enough to cool me down. I was angry. How dare he speak to us that way. It was so *rude*.

"Father wouldn't have stood for that." I folded my arms and trudged along the road, my blood boiling with indignation.

"Your father . . . he was raised different." Grandmother rubbed her forehead at the mention of my father's birth. He was the result of a union between my grandmother and her enslaver, a union that could never be consensual. That fact made her uncomfortable, even though she loved my father. "He spent a lot of time in the big plantation house. He's never known the lash. But I have."

"Grandma, the postman doesn't have a whip behind the counter," I said. At least I thought it was the truth.

"No, but there are worse things than a whip. Why do you think we're safer in numbers? Or why do you think we avoid their eye contact?" She whirled around to face me. "Because we are not safe in white spaces. One wrong word or one sour look, and they'll string you up."

"String us up? There hasn't been a hanging in these parts for ages." My mouth gaped at the thought of it. "Things are changing because they have to change. That's what my father says."

"Girl, I know you are my son's child. Which means you got a hot head. You just be careful with that temper when you are in front of white folks. Things are changing but not that fast." She turned the corner to head up the small dirt road that led to her cottage. She thrust the letters into my hands. "Hold these."

I took them wordlessly and shuffled through the short stack. I didn't see my parents' handwriting or my siblings', so I tucked it under my arm and trudged after Grandmother all the way back to her house.

When we got home, I went straight to the side room, where I'd scooted a kitchen chair near a window. On the nearby table, my book was still resting spine up and splayed out. Determined to transport myself out of my frustrating world, I sat down and resumed reading where I left off.

Only a few moments later, the floorboards in the hallway creaked. I steeled myself, clenching my jaw in preparation for another talking-to. But when I looked up at my grandmother's face, her rosy cheeks had drained of their color. Her lips slackened. She stammered as she lifted the letter to read through it again.

"What is it, Grandma?" I set my book face down on the table. Something told me that this wasn't related to her stern words outside of the post office. This was different. I could feel it. I pushed away from the table and took a small step forward. "Grandma?"

"It's terrible. I don't know what to say."

"Then may I?" I took a few more steps until I was close enough to reach for the letter. "May I read it?"

"Yes, baby." She brushed my cheek as she handed me the paper. She was consoling me for something. It must have been serious.

Bile rose in my throat as I scanned through the letter.

Yellow fever had come to Holly Springs.

I flew across the room in an instant. I needed to pack my things and leave on the first train I could catch. I was a flurry of activity, but my grandmother squeezed my shoulder, halting me.

"You cannot go to Holly Springs. Not when fever is

spreading. And you're just getting over a cold. Don't think I haven't heard your sniffles at night."

"But what if they need my help?"

"The best thing for you to do is stay here and stay safe." My grandmother pursed her lips and looked out the window, like she was considering whether her own advice was sound. After a while she shook her head. "I don't believe we should worry. This is not the first time yellow fever has come to this area. Your parents will weather the storm." She smiled tightly, almost like she was forcing herself to believe it was true. "And if it gets too dangerous for them, I'm sure they will come to the country. You'll see. It will all be well."

I gave a weak smile in return, trying my hardest to believe her.

Chapter 3

MEMPHIS, A SISTER CITY TO HOLLY SPRINGS, had outbreaks of yellow fever several times in the past, but we expected it to fizzle out before it spread to Holly Springs. The mayor, in particular, was not concerned with a full-fledged epidemic. He kept the city open and refused to quarantine the area against new travelers. If he had that much faith, then I should too.

At least, that's what I hoped.

But it niggled at me that I wasn't there to make sure my family was okay. I was the oldest child, and I always felt that I should help care for my younger sisters and brothers. My only hope was that my parents would stay home and have zero contact with anyone outside the household. Either that or they could leave and come to the country. I peered out at the fields, waiting to see their cart coming down the dirt road.

I busied myself around my grandmother's house. It was har-vest time on their farm, and there was no shortage of work. Being productive was the only thing that silenced my dark thoughts.

"How is your fever?" Grandmother touched my forehead with the back of her hand, feeling its slick heat.

"It's better." I tilted my head away from her and continued shucking corn. I was not in the mood to be poked and prod-ded. I had been ill, but I wasn't sick enough to stay in bed.

"Honey, you'll get yourself too worked up over this yel-low fever news, and you won't be able to focus on healing." She sighed and looked out to the fields. "How on earth did you get malaria after only a few weeks?"

"I'll be fine. And after I'm well, maybe I can go home to get my family."

"No, no, we discussed this." She shook her head so hard that the jowls beneath her chin jiggled. "You cannot go there. This summer heat and all the people coming and going through the city—we don't need you getting any sicker." She gave me a pitiful look. "Come and get me if there's any news."

"All right." I nodded and tried to smile, even though I didn't expect to receive any word. It had been several weeks since we received news of the outbreak, but no letters ever came. I was sick with fever but even sicker with worry.

I looked back out to the road, as I frequently did through-out the day, every single day. This time when I looked, I saw three riders blazing down the lane, kicking up dust as their horses galloped toward the house. I blinked in disbelief.

I sprang up and ran to meet them. My stomach twisted into knots. What news would greet me when they arrived? Would my family be safe or . . .

The alternative was too grim to even consider. No, they had to be fine.

The men came to a halt in front of the house and dismounted quickly. I recognized them from Holly Springs.

"Hello." I beamed up at the men, who towered above my small stature. It was good to see familiar faces who surely had news from home.

"Please, come in." My grandmother gestured to the front door, and the riders shuffled into the house. She pulled out her chair and sat down. "Please, have a seat. Ida, get the men something to drink."

I scrambled to the kitchen to get some glasses and the pitcher of tea. I usually found social calls a bit trying, but I was excited to get back to the table.

"Tell me, do you have news from my family?"

"Yes, that is why we're here," said one man as he pulled out a letter from the breast pocket of his coat and handed it to me.

This was what I'd been waiting for.

I ripped open the letter, so eager to hear from my parents that I didn't even excuse myself to go into the other room. I was sure they had written to tell us they were in the country, probably staying with my aunt Belle.

But it was not written by my mother. It wasn't written by

my father, either. It was from our next-door neighbor. It was odd that she was writing me and not my family. The hair on the back of my neck stood up as I read through the note.

About halfway through the page my breath hitched. I had read the most impossible thing I could have possibly imagined.

Jim and Lizzie Wells have both died of the fever. They died within twenty-four hours of each other. The children are all at home.

"What's happened?" My grandmother's desperate voice quivered from across the table. "What's happened to my boy?"

"That can't be. I just saw them," I said in a breathy whisper. "I *just* saw them."

Just then my aunt and uncle ran into the house, breathless from running through the cotton fields. They had seen the three horsemen and wanted to know what was happening. They looked from me to Grandmother, who was silently weeping into her hands.

"My parents are dead," I wailed, wiping my tearstained cheek with the back of my hand. "The fever took them."

Our hopes shattered, my grandmother's home fell into a deep state of mourning.

Chapter 4

MY HEART ACHED IN SUCH A WAY THAT I was sure it would never mend. My eyes burned from shedding so many tears that I began to think they'd always be red and puffy. The only thing that would cure me was to go home and see my surviving family. My siblings, who were under the care of the Howard Association charity, needed their older sister with them.

My family in Tippah County was quite adamant about me waiting a little while longer for the epidemic to dissipate. But I was as determined to travel as they were adamant about me staying. I kissed my grandmother goodbye and made the journey back home in a simple black dress.

There were no passenger trains from Tippah to Holly Springs. And why would there be? No one in their right mind would want to go to the heart of a yellow fever outbreak.

But I wasn't in my right mind. Desperation had gotten the better of my judgment.

I would travel home to my brothers and sisters, come hell or high water.

The journey back to Holly Springs was dimmer and duller than my trip to the country. It was as if everything was grayer now, as if my grief had cast a shadow on the world. I saw the world through this blue lens, and it depressed me. I was traveling on a freight train—the only option—so there were no people to watch or distract me. My eyes had nothing to do but stare at the wall. When the conductor came, he cleared his throat, bringing my attention back to the present.

"Ticket?" he asked in his Southern drawl. When I handed it to him, he tsked under his breath when he saw my destination. "Don't you know there's still fever there? It's a mistake to go to Holly Springs."

I swayed with the jostling of the train, which was draped in black cloth. It honored the two previous conductors who had succumbed to the fever. The current conductor was right to ask me why I was traveling, but he also was marching toward death's door. "Why are you working the train during all this?" I asked.

"Somebody's gotta do this job." He shrugged.

"I also have a job to do." I clenched my jaw, holding my head up straighter.

Sometimes there were hard jobs that still needed to be done. My parents used to say that my job was to go to school and learn everything I could. But now that they were gone, I'd inherited a new job—I needed to take care of the family they could no longer look after.

I returned my quiet yet determined gaze to the wall, feeling the last of my childhood wither away.

I was now the head of my household.

When I got home, my sister Genie was seated in the kitchen in front of the stove. Just weeks ago, I'd seen my mother standing in that very spot, putting her finishing touches on her famous buttermilk biscuits. Now she was gone. I'd never know her secret ingredient for those biscuits. Instead of remembering the taste of her biscuits, I had a bitter taste in my mouth that I could barely swallow.

My eyes welled with tears. They streamed down my face before I had time to wrap my arms around my sister.

"Oh, Ida." She gripped onto my sleeves, her body rumbling as she burst into tears. "I've missed you."

"And I you." My eyes stung with another onslaught of tears. But I stowed them away, releasing the hug to look around the house. It was quiet—too quiet for the always boisterous Wells house. "Where are the children?"

"They're sleeping." My sister's eyes were downcast. "All of them are recovering from the fever. Well, except one."

"Oh my God." I covered my face from the shock. The letter that I'd read at my grandmother's house had only mentioned my parents' passing. It didn't say anything about one of the children dying. "No, don't tell me. Not one of the little ones."

"The baby passed away a couple days ago." Genie sniffled. "Mother tried to nurse him even after she'd fallen ill. But then her milk clotted and she got sicker. Daddy came home and tried to help her fight the fever, but then he got sick."

"And you?" I gripped her hand, feeling her warmth and strength. She was as well as I'd ever seen her, seemingly unscathed from the fever that had ravaged our household. "Did you catch the fever?"

"No, it never touched me." She scrunched up her face and buried her head in her hands. She was sobbing in earnest now, deep, breathy cries that brought me to my knees before her.

"Please don't cry. You'll make me cry more," I said as tears burned my eyes. "I have already cried so much. Please, Genie. Let's be thankful that you're all right."

"How can I be thankful when I blame myself?" Her lips quivered as her whimpers dissipated. "Mother and Father would have moved us all to the country if it wasn't for me. It's difficult for me to travel, because of my legs. And it's difficult to travel with the baby, too. So between the two of us, we chained everybody to this place, this house of death and sorrow."

I let that fact sink in. My parents might have stayed to protect Genie, to keep the family whole instead of leaving her to fend for herself. They did this because family was the most important thing to my parents.

"It's not your fault. It was a judgment call for our parents. And, Genie, we're not alone. Half of Holly Springs may have fled, but that means that the other half stayed. And many of them were the people we know and love."

"Perhaps it was the wrong judgment," Genie said in a soft voice. "And anyway, it doesn't matter anymore, now that we'll be split up."

"What are you talking about?"

"The town Masons are meeting in a few days to decide what's to be done with us. Nothing is decided yet, but I suspect they'll want to rehouse the little ones with an adult. And they'll put me . . ." Her voice hiccuped and she looked away. When she returned her gaze, her eyes were red and her cheeks were tearstained. "They'll put me in the poorhouse. I'm sure of it."

My mischievous sister, who always had a sparkle in her eyes, had nothing but fear in them now. Her scared gaze bored into mine, a stare that told me she'd been agonizing over this for days.

"Don't say that." I looked away from her, afraid she'd see the fear brewing behind my eyes. She was right to be scared. Without parents to protect her, she was vulnerable. We all were.

"It's true," she said and blinked her unshed tears away. "I am of no use to anyone. No one will want me. I'll be cast out."

"Listen to me, Eugenia." I grabbed her shoulders and shook her, trying to snap her back to the present. "*Genie, listen.* You're not going to be discarded. And what are you talking about not being of any use to anyone? You are important to me, to this family."

"You have to say that because you're my sister."

"You know better than anyone—I don't say anything unless I believe it. I try only to speak the truth. You are very important to us. You held this family together."

"I suppose I did help save our money," she said, tilting her head to the side. "When Father died, I caught the nurse going through his pockets. So I entrusted his savings to Dr. Gray. It's in his safe now."

"See? You saved a small fortune for us."

"So maybe you'll retrieve the money from Dr. Gray, and maybe I can stay with you?"

"Of course you're staying with me." I wiped my cheek with the back of my hand. I pictured my parents huddled in our home, defiant until their last breath, determined to keep our family intact. Perhaps that was their dying wish. And I intended to honor it. I heaved myself off the floor and grabbed Genie's hand. "We're all going to stay together. It's what our parents would have wanted, right?"

"I don't know what they would have wanted. We didn't plan for any of this to happen." She turned away and sniffled into her sleeve. "But yes, I suppose you're right. Mama would have wanted us to stay together if at all possible."

"Then it's settled." I nodded resolutely. "I'll get a job. I got good marks in school. There has to be something out there for me."

"You'll have to convince the Masons. Since Father was a Master Mason, they think it's their job to look out for us."

"No. It's my job." I stomped my foot just like my mother used to do when she wanted to make a point. I was grateful for the protection of the Masons. They were a powerful organization of skilled craftsmen, pillars of the community. They would shield us from ruin until we could support ourselves.

But my family was *my* responsibility now.

Chapter 5

BOB MILLER'S BUSHY MUSTACHE WIGGLED as he addressed the Masons gathered in my family home. He leaned forward in his chair and addressed the group.

"It makes sense for the boys to get apprenticeships in James Wells's trade. I have on occasion had the pleasure to observe them in James's workshop, and I think they have inherited some of his carpentry skills."

"Quite right," the Mason to his right said and stroked his beard. "And what is to become of the girls?"

"Uh." Bob's eyes darted toward me and Eugenia, seated opposite him. Our younger sisters were outside. We all awaited our fates. Bob blinked rapidly, then turned toward the rest of the group. "Well, the little ones should go to Mason families. James, didn't you say Nellie expressed a wish to have a child?"

"That's right, she did. And Robert's wife would also like a little girl in her house."

"That's splendid." Bob rubbed his hands together. "The two smallest girls are taken care of."

"And what about us?" I said from my perch. I had remained silent this whole time. I felt like a small schoolgirl—afraid to speak, unsure of what to say. But it was clear now that Eugenia's worst nightmare was about to come true. She was not accounted for in these plans.

"Genie can go to the charitable house until we find a home for her." Bob waved his hand dismissively, as if this were a foregone conclusion. He'd washed his hands of Genie without a moment's hesitation. ". . . although it is likely going to take some time. She will be *challenging* to place."

"And, of course, you are old enough to take care of yourself," James Hall said, assessing me. "Aren't you, girl?"

"Yes, I believe I am." I raised my eyebrow and cocked my head to the side. "I suppose I am an adult now."

"Yes, she is," Bob Miller slapped his knee with his hand. "You are a credit to your parents."

"And since I am an adult, I have something to add to this meeting. If I may?" I waited for Bob to nod in agreement. I nodded, smiling sweetly. "I will take charge of all the children."

"Well . . ." His voice trailed off. He looked nervously from Eugenia to me. "What do you mean?"

"I would like all of my brothers and sisters to remain here in the home that our father built."

"Be sensible." He opened, then closed, his mouth, as if he was confused as to what to say. After a moment he recovered. He leaned forward in his chair, his eyebrows sliding into a stern frown. "You have no means by which to support them. Surely you must understand that raising a family requires money."

"I heard her talking to Dr. Gray the other day." One of the Masons behind Bob pursed his lips, eyeing me suspiciously. "The doctor said something about giving her money."

"Oh . . ." Bob's eyes grew wide. He sat back in his chair.

The men averted their eyes, as if they were ashamed to look upon me. Genie tugged at my sleeve and leaned forward, whispering in my ear, "What is the problem with that? The money is rightfully ours."

"So that is the way you mean to support yourself?" Bob asked. "By asking white men for favors? By inviting them to your home to pay you money?"

Genie deflated beside me, shifting to sit straighter in her seat. She got the gist of what they were saying, and so did I. I squirmed in my seat as I looked around the room at the men who were supposed to be my protectors. They avoided my eye contact, as if they didn't want to be tainted by association.

This is what people thought of me? My parents were not even cold in their graves and already I was falling prey to town gossip. I was a single young woman without protection. I straightened my posture and held up my chin. I would not let them smear my good name.

"Dr. Gray has money for us from our father. Father entrusted him with it when he was on his deathbed. And he's kept it safe all this time." I paused for a moment, trying to calm myself. I could feel my hotheadedness rising. I wanted to shout at the men, but I knew that was not going to get me anywhere. Instead, I spoke quietly but sternly, a tone I'd learned from my mother when she was in her most lethal mood. "There is nothing untoward going on between me and Dr. Gray, and I would appreciate it if you would quash those rumors when you hear them."

"My apologies, ma'am." Bob blinked rapidly, evidently feeling the heat in my voice.

It was the first time I'd ever been called ma'am. It defined me in a way that made my heart flutter. I was the adult head of my household now. I sat up even straighter, bolstered by my small victory over petty gossip.

"The funds from my father will be enough to hold us over until I find a position somewhere suitable," I said.

"Miss Wells seems quite determined," Bob said with a shake of his head. He obviously did not agree with my decision. But he knew he could not sway my stubbornness. "She is just like her father."

"You may want to inquire at the local country schools." James nodded encouragingly. "I've heard they are always looking for capable young women such as yourself."

"James!" Bob raised his eyebrows. His wide eyes looked shocked, like James was helping to shove me off a cliff.

"What? I'm merely providing Ida with a promising lead, that's all." He shrugged while he strolled across the room. "You said it yourself—Ida is basically an adult now."

"And you are decided on this decision?" Bob cocked his head to the side, waiting for my final answer.

"Yes, sir. I am determined to keep my family together. Whatever it takes." I nodded resolutely. "And thank you, Mr. James. I will reach out to the country schools."

"Well, I have made my thoughts known." Bob lifted himself out of his chair and grabbed his hat from the kitchen counter. He was clearly eager to be done with this business, to leave me to my folly. "But I am rather relieved that this matter is settled."

"You and me both," Genie said from her chair near the fireplace. She held her serious face for a few moments, but then her mouth broke into a toothy grin. I smiled back at her.

We were going to stay in our home. We were going to stay together.

Chapter 6

I DID AS MR. JAMES HAD INSTRUCTED AND
inquired at the local country schools to see if I could be
of use. There was indeed interest in my application. My
good marks in school had made me an attractive candidate
for a rural school just outside town. It wasn't exactly a dream
job for me, but I did like that my instruction included reading
and writing. I knew I wanted my future career to have those
components. But teaching small children . . .

Well, at least it was a paying job, and I needed to put my
dreams to the side and provide for my family.

So, at the start of every week, I mounted a mule and rode
slowly to school. On the weekends I came home and did a
long list of chores, including cooking for the week.

I stood over the kitchen stove, watching the tiny bubbles
pop through the grits, waiting for them to be just right. I

dipped my spoon into the pot and stirred it around, making sure the grits wouldn't stick to the bottom of the cast iron. Then I brought the spoon to my lips and blew some of the heat off before putting it in my mouth. They were good. Almost as good as my mother's.

My chest swelled with pride as Genie scooted toward me and heaved herself into a kitchen chair.

"You'll want to check the oven." She scrunched up her face, looking to the old iron oven. Her nose crinkled. "I think they've been in there a bit too long."

"Oh no." I crouched in front of the door and swung it open. My umpteenth attempt at making biscuits had had a promising start. But they were now a dark brown, scorched from baking too long. "I was so focused on everything else that I forgot they were in there."

"You'll get the hang of it soon enough." She flashed a placating smile. "I have every confidence."

The front door swung open, and my grandmother walked in with a handful of eggs from the coop behind the house. She'd come in from the country to help with the children while I worked during the week. I may have convinced the Masons that I was an adult and was able to run my own household, but the truth was more complicated.

I was overwhelmed. I needed the guidance of a learned hand.

When Grandmother heard that I would be shouldering the burden of having six mouths to feed, she sent word that she would come and stay with us for a while. She would help while I worked at my new position.

Now Grandmother's nostrils puckered, and she sniffed toward the stove. "Is something burning?"

"It's nothing," Genie muttered from her seat at the table.

"It's all right, Genie. I can own my mistakes when I make them." I stepped to the side, revealing the overcooked biscuits.

"I told you to keep an eye on them." Grandma tutted as she walked over to the stove. She poked one of them with her finger.

"You also instructed me to keep the oven closed as much as possible so that I wouldn't let the heat out." I sighed and looked at the clock.

"It's all right. I can manage here." Grandma shooed me away with her hands. She pointed toward the door, where my travel bag waited on the floor. "It's about time you get going."

"Thank you, Grandmother." I clasped her wrinkly hands in mine. She was in her seventies, and still she traveled to Holly Springs to take care of the children while I worked at the country school. "You've been a godsend."

"Oh, I almost forgot." Grandma held her finger up as she rummaged around in her apron pocket. "Your aunt Fanny has written. She has invited you all to come to Memphis. There is a school there in need of a teacher."

My aunt was eager to unite our two families in the city. I knew this because she had written about it a few times. She had lost her husband in the same yellow fever epidemic that took my parents and baby Stanley. Left with three small children to raise on her own, she wanted the closeness of family. Aunt Fanny was very persistent when she had her mind set on something.

It was a tempting prospect. Working in a city school would provide more income than the mere twenty-five dollars a month I earned. It would also provide opportunities to mingle with society and meet new and exciting people.

The country itself didn't have much to offer. A one-room schoolhouse with dingy walls was all I had to house my students. The residents were much friendlier than I expected. But in all honesty, I didn't enjoy my placement much. Memphis could be a nice change in pace.

But since I had just started the school term, I was stuck. My father had always said a man was only as good as his reputation. I figured it was the same way for women. I had to fulfill my commitment to my current school.

"Please thank her for the offer," I said, hesitating, trying to find a diplomatic answer. "I will consider it for next term."

"All right." Grandmother brought her hand to her head. Her knees buckled beneath her and she gripped the table to steady herself.

"Grandma!" I leapt forward, throwing my arms out to provide support.

"I'm all right." She waved her hand weakly. "Please don't fuss. Just got a bit lightheaded, that's all."

Genie snuck a look at me, panicked. I'm sure my face

reflected the same fear I saw in hers. We needed Grandma's
help. She helped hold the family together while I was teaching.
Eugenia was a big help, but there was only so much she could
do. But my position in the country only worked if Grandma
was watching the children while I was away. And by the look
of her pale face, Grandma wasn't fit for anything but bed rest.

"I should write to the school and tell them I can't come in
tomorrow," I said as I unbuttoned my coat.

"You will do no such thing." Grandma held her hand up. "I
am *fine*. Just need to sit for a spell. That's all this is."

"Okay." My voice trailed off. I wanted to believe that
she was fine. But her pallor told a different story. I looked to
Eugenia, who gave me a reassuring nod. What passed between
us was an unspoken promise that she would keep an eye on
Grandma and make sure everything was, in fact, *fine*. I held
fast to that reassurance and grabbed my shawl from the hook
behind the door. "Okay, I'm off then. There's some butter and
eggs in the cabinet. Teachers and parents are always giving me
food to take home. They want to make sure everyone's fed."

"We'll eat well, I promise," Genie said, nodding to the
stove with a sly smirk. "Starting with your biscuits."

My mule shuffled her feet almost the entire six miles to
the country school just outside town. Periodically, she
strayed from the road when she saw patches of grass perfect
for munching. Normally, I indulged her on our quiet rides
through the country. I wanted to stay on her good side since

she was my only means of transportation. But I tugged her back toward the road. It was getting late, and I didn't want to be on the roads after dark.

When I pulled the reins in front of my lodgings, she grumbled but complied. I patted her mane and then dismounted.

During the week, I lived near the school in a quaint but well-kept house just off the main road. It was much smaller than my childhood home. But this was the country, not Holly Springs.

I was not unhappy. No, I was grateful for the position. It afforded me the ability to take care of my family. But Grandmother wasn't going to last much longer. Her health was poor, and she deserved to rest for whatever time she had left on this earth.

Sooner or later, I would need to move back to town. Or to a city.

As I walked into the house, I resolved to study for the city examination so that I could teach in the public schools in Memphis. There was more that this world had to offer me than a quiet country life.

And I aimed to seize the opportunity. This was my destiny.

I had been so focused on the day-to-day role of caring for my family that I hadn't thought much beyond that. But this job provided hope, and I felt the flicker of opportunity pass through me.

Chapter 7

A GENTLE NUDGE THREATENED TO ROUSE me from my slumber, but I fought against it. A harder shove on my shoulder ripped me from sleep. I woke with a start, blinking to clear my eyes and see the world around me. I had fallen asleep at the kitchen table, surrounded by books and papers and kitchen prep. A bucket of damp clothes sat to the right of my chair.

Genie's face glowed by the candlelight; her soft features hardened with a frown. She set her candle on the table and sighed. "You can't go on like this."

"I don't know what you mean," I said as haughtily as I could muster.

"Ida!" She tilted her head to the side with a tsk. "You run yourself more ragged every week. You take care of your students in the country. You even take care to mentor their *parents* by giving them advice on practical things. And then you come home and you make sure everyone's needs are met except your own."

I didn't do her the disservice of lying and saying she was wrong. I folded my arms and looked away from her. Oddly, the image of the weary train conductor came to mind. I adopted his reasoning for being on a fever-riddled train route as my reason for being at the head of this family. "Somebody has to do this job."

"Not at this cost," Genie said, reaching for my hand. I slid it off the table, just out of her reach. "I won't see you run yourself into the ground like Grandmother did."

"Genie, that's different. Nothing seems to go easily, so it should have been expected." A hollow chuckle escaped from my chest. "Grandmother collapsed from all the overwork on top of her old age."

I had long given up on the dream of restoring my family to its former glory, to the happy, boisterous home it once was. It was all about survival now.

"You will end up the same way—collapsed on the floor—if you don't listen to me." Genie gritted her teeth, setting her jaw into a hard line. She was serious now, and she insisted on my full attention. "When our aunt came to retrieve Grandmother and her things, she asked you to consider moving to Memphis. I think you should go."

"What do you think I'm doing here?" I gestured to all the books in front of me. "I am studying for the city school exam."

"Yes, but you can still teach in the schools right outside of Memphis while you're studying for the test. It pays more than what you're making now. And you'd be near trains and trollies and people your own age."

"Keep your voice down." I shushed her with a hiss. I didn't want her to wake the girls, who were fast asleep.

She painted a tantalizing picture. I'd be lying if I said I hadn't thought of the opportunities Memphis had to offer.

"See? You want to leave." Genie folded her arms, a smug smile sneaking across her lips.

"But what about you? Are you able to make the journey?"

"That's the thing. I don't think I'll go with you." Genie's eye twitched like she might cry, but she looked away before I could see her eyes pool with tears. She continued, her voice thick with emotion, "Aunt Belle said I can stay with her, and we will look after Jim and George. They are apprenticed and finding their way. They don't need much help these days."

"You want to divide and conquer." I nodded slowly as comprehension sank in. "I'll take Annie and Lily with me to Memphis."

"And I'll stay here with the boys." My sister nodded. "And Aunt Belle will help watch over them too."

"It would mean more money." My eyebrows upturned. Genie was right about all of it, but I couldn't help but think I was failing. "I tried. I really tried to keep us all together."

"You *did* keep the family together. And we're forever grateful that you stood in the gap that mother and father left."

"But must I always part with the ones I love?" My lip quivered as I wrapped my arms around my sister. "I don't want to leave you."

Holly Springs was my home. This house was the house that my mother and father had built together—and eventually, they had died together in this house. I wanted to secure a better position closer to the city and society. I wanted to be closer to opportunity. But when I allowed myself to truly consider Memphis as a viable option, I felt a fresh wave of grief at leaving this house—and those still in it—behind.

Deep down I knew that if I left Holly Springs, I'd never come back to live here.

I released Genie from our hug and crossed the room. It was as if my parents were infused in this house. I laid my palms on the walls, grieving their loss all over again as I whimpered.

And then I peeled myself off the wall and wiped my nose with the back of my hand. I steadied myself, straightened my back, and stared into Genie's eyes. "I'm not ready to say goodbye to you. I'll think about moving to Memphis, but not yet. I need more time."

"Don't take too much time. Life is short, Ida."

Chapter 8

THINGS NEVER GOT BETTER IN HOLLY SPRINGS. After my grandmother went back to the country, a family friend agreed to stay with my siblings during the weekdays. The travel and the work were exhausting, and sometimes the depression was so overwhelming, I felt as if I would shatter into a million pieces. But nothing compared to the deep feeling of grief that came with Eugenia's death. She was too young to leave us, but her health grew worse and worse with each passing month. It felt as though death kept coming for the Wells family, and Genie's death made one thing very clear to me: I had to leave Holly Springs. Genie got her wish.

My brothers stayed in Mississippi with Aunt Belle, and Annie, Lily, and I moved to Memphis, Tennessee. It took me years to pass the city school examination, but once I did, it offered me more teaching opportunities. We lodged with my aunt Fanny and her children in her small house at 62 Georgia Street in South Memphis, and while I was at school, my aunt helped take care of my sisters.

Eventually, I began teaching at Saffarans Street School, which was located in a large brick building in the city, with large classrooms. But even if the building was large, the class sizes were still overcrowded like they were in my other schools, so my new position came with its challenges.

But I was older and wiser than the girl who rode a mule to class years ago. I knew how to get a rowdy class to pay attention.

I slapped my ruler against my desk. The crack sliced through my students' late afternoon chatter. They turned in their seats, facing forward. I waited a moment as they all looked at me quietly.

"All right, class. You'll need to finish your reading by first thing next week. Class dismissed."

My students shuffled out of the classroom at the end of the day, some grumbling under their breath about how I was a hard teacher. I didn't mind it in the slightest. My assignments were designed to shape young minds into productive members of society. I did not coddle my students, even though they were young. The world would not coddle them either.

I knew that fact better than most.

"You're settling in nicely, I see," a fellow teacher said, leaning against my door frame.

"I'd like to think so." I very much liked it here. But I had fallen prey to petty gossip at school and in town. As hard as I worked to be a productive member of society, I was still a single woman with two young girls. My situation invited talk.

I wondered if this teacher's visit to my classroom was a friendly one. I was guarded as I continued. "If you have any advice for me, I would welcome it."

"No, we all think you're marvelous." The woman shrugged and let out an airy laugh. "Your students seem so engaged and enthusiastic. Which is sometimes hard to achieve. I salute you."

"Uh, thank you." I blinked in surprise. "I'm Ida, and you are?"

"Oh, yes, of course. I'm Fannie." She stepped into my classroom with an outstretched hand. When she took mine in hers, she shook it with a vigor that made me feel like it was genuine. "I teach just down the hall over there."

"That's my aunt's name," I said. "I surely won't forget it. Nice to meet you."

"Listen, would you like to join our lyceum?" she asked encouragingly. "I guess you could say it's our little club of teachers."

"That sounds interesting." I smiled politely, still feeling slightly guarded. I had never been so welcomed in my short teaching career. And I had not yet found my peers— somewhere I felt I truly belonged. I wasn't sure if this was it. "What do you do in your club?"

"We read essays and recite poetry. We also listen to music whenever someone with an instrument comes to grace us." She leaned forward, her eyes sparkling mischievously. She instantly reminded me of Genie. "And we always seem to find time for the *Evening Star.* You familiar with it?"

"Of course." I nodded emphatically. It was one of my favorite weekly newspaper reads. The articles were feisty and their columns were even spicier. I loved to see the expression of our people in the written word. "I particularly like the They Say column."

"We do too." Fannie clasped her hands and beamed. "Tell me that you'll join us next Friday afternoon."

"I don't see why not."

"Splendid," Fannie said and shoved off my desk. "We meet at the Vance Street Christian Church. Do you know it? It's the one with the white steeple?"

"Yes, I know it." I nodded, conjuring a picture of it in my mind. It was just off the streetcar line.

"The very one." Fannie retreated backward, waving excitedly. "See you Friday."

I waved back, my jaw a bit slackened.

My chest swelled with hope. I had just made a friend.

Meeting people in Memphis had proved to be more difficult than I'd ever imagined. I didn't have the easy, carefree personality I'd had in my youth that made it possible to form relationships. That butterfly schoolgirl had been whittled down by the blunter edge of womanhood. After all I had been through, I now possessed an intensity that served as my compass in life.

And there also was the fact that I didn't enjoy my work. Most of my peers thought that teaching was their calling in life. I did not.

Teaching was a means to an end, a way to fulfill my obligation to provide for my family. My heart just wasn't in it. Sure, I was grateful for my job at Saffarans Street School because it paid almost twice as much as the country schools and because it saved me from a job as a maid or domestic servant for some rich family. But my gratitude ended there. I feared that if I continued down this teaching path too long, I'd be pigeonholed in it for the rest of my life.

I wanted to do more with my life. The urgency I felt when I was younger was back.

My head was swimming with these wistful thoughts as I stepped onto the ladies' car on the train and sat down in my seat. It cost thirty cents for a first-class car ticket, but I preferred it to the other cars, which were filled with drunkards and the prying eyes of men, who often preyed on young women. The ladies' car was away from the other crowded cars and downstream from the coal smoke from the engine. The seats had plush cushions on them. This was a small luxury I gifted myself.

My time on the train allowed me to be by myself, which wasn't something I often had. Between my full schoolroom and my aunt's house full of children and noise, I seldom had a quiet moment alone. I filled this quiet train time reading. I'd read Genie's copy of *Little Women* several times, but I always came back to it. I loved the fierce independence of those girls, Jo in particular. But today I chose to read a newspaper and to catch up on local events.

"Ticket?" The conductor wiggled his fingers at me, awaiting my first-class pass.

"Yes, sir." I handed him my ticket without taking my eyes off my book.

"I can't take your ticket here."

"Don't you take tickets at the seats?" I asked, looking up from my book.

"You will have to go to the car ahead of this one." He pointed to the front of the train. "That is where you can find your seat and I'll take your ticket there."

"But that's a smoking car." I craned my head around the seat and looked down the aisle toward the window of the adjoining car. It was filled with smoke. "I prefer to keep my seat here, thank you."

"Come on, you. Don't make trouble for me." The conductor grabbed my arm and yanked me toward him.

I shrank against the wall and braced my boots around the seat in front of me as I struggled to stay put. But he reached for my other arm and pulled harder.

I acted out of pure instinct. I clamped my teeth around the back of his hand and bit him. Hard.

"Ow!" The man pulled back his arm and shook it, obviously trying to shake the pain away. His upturned eyebrows were indignant as he gawked at me. "What'd you do that for?"

"How dare you manhandle me!" I covered my mouth. My hands were shaking. I was in shock.

The man left in a huff, stumbling back down the aisle toward the rear door. My shaking hands tried to straighten out my dress, which was ruffled and wrinkled from the scuffle. When I looked up, everyone in the compartment was craning their necks over their seats to stare at me.

They'd seen me be molested by the conductor. They should have been sympathetic to my predicament, outraged, even. But instead, their eyes and frowns looked accusatory. They were blaming me for the disturbance. That much was clear.

My cheeks heated and I looked away from them. I couldn't help the creeping sense of shame that flooded over me. I inwardly chastised myself for feeling ashamed of being *me*. I hadn't done anything wrong. I had purchased a ticket for this car. I hadn't done anything to provoke the conductor's actions. All I had done was live in this world as a Black woman.

That alone can get you into trouble.

I leaned forward as the train jerked to a stop at the next station. I snuck a glance at the woman in front of me. Her eyes were trained on the rear train door. The hair on the back of my neck stood up as I felt a breeze brush against me. The door to our compartment was open, and multiple pairs of footsteps thudded toward me. The conductor was coming back to finish yanking me from my seat, and he'd brought help.

I hooked my feet around the chair in front of me, bracing myself once again.

"This the one?" a man asked. I recognized him as the baggage man who had helped me onto the train.

"Of course," said one of the passengers, who rose from his seat to help the conductor.

"All right, up you get." The conductor wrapped his fingers around my upper arm and my wrist.

"That's it." The baggage man and the passenger grunted beside him as he threaded his hands beneath my armpits and then pulled upward.

Of course, I could not match the strength of three fully grown men. My foothold on the seat in front of me dislodged as I was lifted out of my seat entirely. My dress sleeve ripped, making a tearing sound. I stopped my struggling and relented to the brute force.

People in my train car were fully gawking at the unfolding scene. Some even knelt on their seats so that they had a better view.

Not a single one protested on my behalf. No one lifted a finger to help me.

As the men carried me down the aisle, ripping my sleeves

at the seams, I scowled back at my fellow passengers, disgusted by them all.

A woman toward the front of the car started to clap. And then quickly she was joined by another and another until the whole car erupted in cheers, thanking the train staff for carrying my offending presence away.

The men dumped me unceremoniously onto the platform.

"I trust you can find your way to the correct car." The conductor sneered while he straightened his uniform coat. He pointed to the car ahead of the women's car. "It's that smoking car right there."

"I'd rather stay here than ride any farther with the likes of you."

"Suit yourself." He shrugged. He rubbed his hand, right where I'd bitten him. "No matter. The train will run without your disruptions."

He waved his arm to the front of the train. It slowly pushed away from the station.

I patted my body, assessing the damage. I was sure to have bruises tomorrow. And I'd need to stay up late tonight in order to sew my dress back together.

My eyes stung with tears. People were already staring at my disheveled appearance. I didn't care if I cried in public right now. My fingers grazed my front pocket. I dove into it, and much to my surprise, I found my ticket.

How I managed to hold on to it, I didn't know. But it was

a boon to my mood. It was a sign that God was looking out for me. I wouldn't have to pay for another fare. I could just hop on the next train.

I hobbled over to the ticket counter to find out when the next train was due to arrive.

Chapter 9

I WAS BEDRAGGLED BY THE TIME I TURNED THE front door handle and stepped inside my aunt's house. Annie and Aunt Fanny were seated at the kitchen table, laughing quietly so as not to wake my aunt's children and Lily. Their smiles soured as they appraised my disheveled appearance. Aunt Fanny shot up from the table so quickly that she nearly knocked her chair over.

"What's happened?" She rushed over to me, holding her arms out as if she thought I might collapse and she'd have to catch me.

"The ticket collector threw me off the train." My shoes scuffed against the wood floor as I hobbled over to the kitchen table.

"Did you do something to upset him?" Annie asked quietly. It wasn't necessarily an accusation, but it did sound cagey and apprehensive. In a lower voice she said, "I know how hot you run sometimes."

It was true that I didn't possess an obedient disposition. Sometimes I wished I was more tractable, more compliant. But I was the head of my house, and I was my father's daughter after all. I made good trouble.

But today, I hadn't done anything wrong. I was certain of that.

"You don't have to do much to get on their bad sides these days," My aunt thankfully chimed in. "They tried to seat you in the smoking compartment, right?"

"Yes!" I took a deep breath, relieved that I didn't have to defend myself. "I was minding my business in the ladies' car, and when I handed the man my ticket, he refused to take it. I refused to move. And next thing I know, I'm being lifted above the seats and tossed onto the platform of the next station."

"There's talk of drawing a color line," Aunt Fanny said grimly. "Having an official separation between the races."

"That is absurd." I threw my hands up and brought them down to slap my hips. "What did father talk about all those nights on the porch with the Masons and men of the community? They worked hard to live in an equal society."

I wanted to sit at the kitchen table and brush off the whole incident, but my stubbornness wouldn't allow me. Something else wouldn't allow me to sit, either. It was urgency. It was an urgent feeling that I had to set things right.

I strode across the room to my desk and snatched my

notebook out of the top drawer. Only when I had my fountain pen in hand was I ready to sit down. I scribbled furiously, almost forgetting about my aunt and sister seated just over my shoulder at the kitchen table.

"Ida, what on earth are you doing?" Aunt Fanny asked.

"I'm writing it all down. Everything that happened on the train—it's going here, on this piece of paper."

"What are you doing that for?" Annie asked with a slight edge to her voice. "Wouldn't you rather just forget the whole thing rather than dwell on it?"

"Nonsense." I tsked under my breath. "I'll need to account for every detail if I'm to bring suit against the railroad."

"Bring suit?" Aunt Fanny's voice cracked as it ticked up a few octaves. "You can't sue the railroad!"

"I most certainly can and will, thank you very much." My lip jutted out in a pout as I continued scribbling. "They can't get away with treating passengers like they treated me today."

"You are your father's child through and through." Aunt Fanny sighed and strummed her fingernails against the table. "I suppose he would have taken a stand."

"And Mother would have too. Don't forget how principled she was."

They both watched me scribble for a few minutes.

"Emancipation, equality, justice—they're not just words on a paper. They have to mean something." I turned in my seat to look at my sister, who was growing up into a young woman. I wanted to instill in her the same fire my parents instilled in me. "Those words have to protect me from being molested in public like that."

"I will miss this," my aunt said, wiping her brow and shaking her head as she watched me write. She sounded wistful. "I will miss your fire."

"Miss it? I suspect it'll take quite some time for all of this to play out in the courts. I'm sure there will be many twists and turns along the way. That's how the legal system is. So you'll have nothing to miss."

There was a pause, and I looked up at Aunt Fanny.

"It's only that I've heard of an opportunity in California, south of San Francisco. And, well, I am considering it." Aunt Fanny snuck a glance at Annie, whose head hung low, as if she'd just received bad news.

"You would move to *California*?" My pen dropped to the desk. I was too stunned to write another word.

"Yes, Ida. That's what she is saying," Annie sighed.

"Of course, it wouldn't be right away. And I'm sure we could find you and the children suitable lodging."

"I don't know if I make enough money to lodge Annie, Lily, and myself." My gaze grew distant as I tabulated my meager financials. Money was stretched as far as it could be, and there still wasn't enough. I couldn't imagine making ends meet without my aunt's support.

"We don't have to speak about this now, since it's so late," Aunt Fanny said. She cleared her throat. "But I could take the girls with me."

It took me a second to realize what she was proposing: taking Annie and Lily with her to California.

"You mean split the family up even further?" I slouched onto my desk, defeated. "Isn't that what I fought so hard to prevent?"

"You have done such a tremendous job, better than anyone dreamed possible. The boys have both found apprenticeships. The girls have continued their education, and they're really a delight. And you are a force to be reckoned with. Ida, you have discharged your duty to your parents beautifully." I didn't know what to do at that point.

"Oh, come here," said Aunt Fanny.

She raised her arms, beckoning me toward her. I crossed the room cautiously, trying to mask my feelings. But she could tell I was upset at this news. She brushed my hair out of my face, just the way my mother used to do. I'd lost her, and now I'd lose my aunt to California.

"I know it's not what you want to hear. But perhaps this will be a good thing. The girls can be with my children who are close in age." She ducked her head so that she could look into my downcast eyes. "And maybe this will give you time to be social. Get out and meet people. Be young and social. Maybe even meet a possible suitor."

"Who has time for courting?" I shrank away from her touch.

"Think about it," she said with a sigh. "All hearts need love to survive."

And then she blew out the candle.

Chapter 10

THERE WAS NOTHING TO THINK ABOUT. Aunt Fanny was moving to California, and there was nothing I could do to stop her. I suppose I could have tried to keep Annie and Lily with me. But our life with Aunt Fanny and her children was somewhat subsidized with shared meals and a shared roof. Without her, our finances would be razor-thin—too thin to provide for the girls in the way they deserved. And deep down, I knew that the girls were better off with her than they were with me. I had to let them go.

As the seasons changed, so did my life. Aunt Fanny and the girls went on to their next adventure out west, leaving me alone in Memphis. My family was fractured. The loss of my Memphis family ties was compounded with years of Holly Springs sadness. I felt these losses keenly. My heart hurt. And there was nothing I could do to bring them back. Aunt Fanny reminded me that I could join them in California; in fact, it was what she truly wanted. I didn't want to leave Memphis, but my loyalty to my sisters and the promise to keep my remaining family together weighed on me constantly. The sadness was suffocating.

To take the sting out of this new season of change, I decided to accept my new friend Fannie Thompson's invitation to engage with the teachers' lyceum.

I was reluctant at first to attend the lyceum. It was comprised mostly of teachers who were no doubt excited about their vocation, true believers in the field of education. And while I certainly understood and appreciated the importance of education—after all, I was a prime example of what a well-educated woman could accomplish—I didn't love the act of teaching. Honestly, I found it to be rather tedious. I was not sure if I would really fit in with this crowd, and I didn't know what to expect, but I wanted to be out and be social.

I walked up the stone steps of Vance Street Christian Church. The ceilings were tall and the hallway was wide. This was a grand old church. My mother, a strongly devout Christian woman, would have dropped to her knees then and there and said a prayer of gratitude. And she would chastise me for not having found a permanent church home yet. I dutifully attended church on Beale Street and the surrounding areas, but I'd yet to find a pastor who I didn't think was a toady, pompous fool who couldn't string two words together.

"Good evening, ma'am," a minister said as he strode down the hall.

I blushed and then patted my hair down. I was thankful he couldn't hear my thoughts.

"If you're here for the lyceum, they are just at the end of the hall."

"Thank you, sir." I nodded politely, wondering if he was, in fact, one of the toads. I followed the path prescribed by the minister, and soon I was standing in the doorway of the church meeting room.

"I'm so glad you came," Fannie said and took me around to show me the seating area. She gestured to an empty chair behind her. "This seat is yours if you want it."

"Of course. But first I think I'll get a glass of water."

I walked over to the small refreshment table. There was a stack of pamphlets on the table and a small donation jar beside it. I took one, then opened my pocketbook for the change to pay for it. I looked into my almost empty satchel.

I was nearly broke.

Even though I no longer had six mouths to feed, I could still scarcely make ends meet. With Aunt Fanny gone, I had to find other accommodations that were less refined and nearly twice the price. I never seemed to have enough money left over to buy anything for myself.

I was setting the weekly paper back on the table when my friend called from the seating area.

"It looks like Ida is eager to be the first reader." She smiled at me, then turned to address the other ladies seated. "Everyone, this is Ida Wells. She taught at Saffarans Street School and now has a position at the Grant Street School. She is already a favorite amongst the pupils."

"You exaggerate." I ducked my head down, feeling embarrassed. If she only knew how much I loathed teaching, she would not give me such praise. I felt like a fraud in front of all these strangers.

"Well, go on then." Fannie twiddled her fingers. "What's the news today?"

I looked down, realizing I still had the newspaper in my hand.

"There's one about General Grant," I said tentatively.

"Go on."

"'A meeting of ex-federal soldiers was held at the Knights of Pythias Hall last evening, looking to make arrangements for the proper observance of Gen. Grant's funeral.

'The meeting was called to order by Capt. Alf. G. Tuther, who stated that as this was not a regular meeting of the Grand Army of the Republic, but a meeting of all ex-Federal soldiers, to make arrangements to attend the obsequies of Gen. Grant, in conjunction with the ex-Confederate soldiers, he moved that J. B. Aldrich be called to the chair, which motion was carried—'

"Goodness, what a mouthful," I said, laughing awkwardly as I folded my paper in my lap. "I always think that speaking plainly is a virtue. Why use a word like *obsequies* when you could just as easily say funeral service?"

"I couldn't agree more," a woman across from me said. "It would make the paper more accessible to people who have difficulty reading."

"I taught in some country schools before finding a position here," I said. "People are desperate to read something that reflects real life and speaks to their concerns, like their concerns about education for Black children."

I thought about the dismal overall attendance numbers at the country schools.

"My classes are large and overcrowded, but that is because Black schools are relegated to smaller, lower quality schoolhouses compared to their white counterparts. In addition to this separate and unequal treatment, a good number of Black students are not enrolled in school. That means there are many children who aren't receiving a formal education. There are so many of us who are struggling to read—parents and children alike."

I looked up and wondered if I had said too much. I didn't know any of these people. I had come in earnest, wanting to make friends.

"It sounds like *you* should write a column then," Fannie said with a smile as she pointed a mischievous finger at me. In that moment, I thought of Eugenia doing the same thing to me. I gulped back the pang of homesickness and grief. Genie had died far too young. And I missed her terribly.

"Don't be silly. I am not particularly gifted with words," I said.

"Not to contradict you, but I think you're being too modest." The women in the room nodded in agreement.

Fannie hardly knew me, but she somehow pegged me accurately. I wrote almost every night in my journal and expressed myself in many regular letters home. I needed a creative outlet to express my thoughts and opinions. I felt trapped. Could my new friend sense that? Did she know that teaching wasn't fulfilling those needs?

"The editor of the *Evening Star* just vacated his post. And they are desperate to find a suitable replacement." Fannie nodded encouragingly. When I hesitated, she threw her hands up. "Oh, come on. There is no harm in paying the journal a visit. I'm sure you have a decent shot."

I thought of all the books I read, all those characters that felt like old friends. Then I thought of my deepest wish to read books with characters that reflected my experience, my corner of existence. I could not have been alone in this wish. Looking around the room, I saw hope reflected in the teachers' eyes. Could I help grant that wish? Not just for me, but for all these women seeking that voice? I couldn't help but feel a sense of urgency, and a glimmer that I could fulfill that urgency this one time. Looking around at these faces, I resolved to find out if I had what it took to write our stories at the paper.

"All right. I'll apply for the post."

Chapter 11

A FEW WEEKS LATER, I SAT IN THE DINING room of my boarding house and beamed at a letter that had just arrived. I could scarcely believe my eyes. I scanned the letter again, and my grin grew wider. The *Evening Star* wanted to fill their editorial vacancy with me.

"What has you grinning ear to ear?" my landlady, Mrs. Hill, asked. She had crept behind me, trying to read my letter over my shoulder.

"Nothing," I said, quickly folding the page and tucking it underneath my breakfast plate.

"A girl like you, who always has a stern look about her, breaks into a smile over breakfast. No, that's not *nothing*." Her eyes narrowed as she rounded the table. I avoided her eye contact, giving her no hint of my news. She could be a difficult woman, and I did not want to discuss anything with her—

not on a day like this. She turned her sights on Ella, a fellow lodger who was just a girl. "Go on then, eat your breakfast."

"Just the one slice of bread for me this morning, ma'am," Ella said in her soft voice.

"Hmm." Mrs. Hill huffed and then scuffled out the kitchen door.

"So," Ella whispered, leaning over the table, "are you going to share the news? Mrs. Hill is many foolish things, but she is a keen observer. I noticed your joy too."

"What did I miss?" Boots, the other boarder, asked as he bustled into the dining room. His eyes looked puffy and his shirt was wrinkled, as if he had just rolled out of bed. "Why is it so quiet in here? Did Mrs. Hill go off on you again?"

"Does the sun rise in the east?" Ella said with a smirk. "I ought to tell my mother about her. But I dare not. There aren't many suitable options for lodging, not at this price."

"You get what you pay for," I grumbled and took a bite of my toast. I did not like lodging here, but it was all I had. I knew well enough what Ella spoke about—there weren't many places in town that were suitable for a respectable young woman to live. I had scoured the city for this place. The rent was a whopping ten dollars a month. On top of that, I sent ten dollars a month to my sisters and aunt in California. And I also sent money to my brothers back home. After that, I had mere pocket change. I had nowhere else to go, and from what I could gather, Ella and Boots had no other options either.

"Oh, do tell us what's in that letter you're hiding." Ella folded her arms with a pout.

"All right then, but don't tell the old toad." I cocked my head toward the kitchen door, where I hoped Mrs. Hill wasn't eavesdropping. She'd have me packing my bags if she heard me referring to her as an amphibian. "I've just received news from the *Evening Star*, and they want to hire me on as a writer. They want me to begin straightaway."

"Oh, that is wonderful news!" Ella clapped her hands.

"Shh, keep quiet." Boots held his finger up to his lips. He nodded at me. "You'll be paid and everything?"

"Of course I will. I will continue teaching while I write for the paper. But some extra money could go a long way."

"Then you're right to keep this quiet." Boots narrowed his eyes. "If Mrs. Toad catches wind of this, she may raise your rent."

And then we all burst into laughter.

That evening, I sat in my small room in the boarding house, holding a pen in my hand. I had set aside my personal journal and my stack of correspondence. I wanted to focus on my first article for the *Evening Star*. But where to begin?

I had observed such a lack of training among the folks in the country. There was of course mending clothing and being presentable, but there were also other issues that plagued country folk and city folk alike—the pervasive discrimination that was creeping back into local politics. The sun had set on the Radical Reconstruction days of my parents' time, where equality wasn't just written on paper but was a living, breathing ideal for us to strive toward.

I wanted to write about voting laws across Tennessee. Although Black men in Memphis could still cast their ballots, all around us there were poll taxes and literacy tests that shut most Black voters out of the political process.

And why were only men allowed to vote? Women were as much a part of a functioning society, and we should have had a say in how our governments ran. I wanted to write about the growing suffrage movement and carve a place out for Black women to be heard and included.

There were so many things I wanted to write.

But I sank back in my chair, grabbing my fountain pen as I considered my course of action. This was a big opportunity, and I didn't want to squander it.

It wouldn't do me any good to submit something fiery and controversial straight out of the starting blocks.

I needed to ease into this slowly.

That's what my mother would have counseled me to do. She also would have counseled me to finish my chores before I settled into my desk. The pile of laundry that was in my room would have displeased her. I took a page out of my mother's book and decided to start with practical advice for everyday life.

Chapter 12

MONTHS LATER, FANNIE AND I WALKED
through the streets of Memphis. We were on our
way to the teacher's lyceum, climbing the steps
of the Vance Street Christian Church.

"I'm telling you, you're a success." Fannie bounced excitedly on the balls of her feet.

"You're being generous, as always." I waved my hand dismissively. But inwardly, my stomach was doing cartwheels.
I was a girl from a small town who had no formal literary
training, and I was a *success*.

That was confirmed when we walked into the lyceum.
The last time I'd been here, the room was half empty. Now
the attendance had doubled. There weren't enough chairs to
seat everyone, which meant that people would have to stand
during the night's readings of the *Evening Star*.

"See?" Fannie nudged me with her elbow. "I told you you were a success."

"Okay, I believe you now."

"You must be the famous Ida B. Wells," said a large man, who took off his hat and gave me a curt bow. "I am so delighted to make your acquaintance."

"You have me at a disadvantage," I said, tilting my head to the side. "With whom do I have the pleasure of speaking?"

"I am Reverend Countee. I am the pastor of one of the biggest Baptist churches in the area."

"The reverend runs a paper of his own called the *Living Way*." Fannie smiled.

"Yes, of course. I do admire your paper. I read it every chance I get. In fact, I saw that you included some of my writings last week."

"It got such a positive response from our subscribers. Actually, I was wondering if you'd consider writing some pieces for my paper."

"Oh, I don't know where I would find the time. I still have school to teach and I write the advice column once a week as is."

"We would very much like you to write for us too." He pursed his lips as he considered his offer. "How about once weekly?"

"Once a week!" Fannie's eyes were wide open.

It was intriguing. The *Living Way* had a larger readership than the *Evening Star*. This could open up more opportunities.

And it would gain me more readership, which would allow me to help more people. I thought for a minute. Could I write for both? Should I write for both? My mind raced. More. I wanted to do more.

"I'd love to," I said.

"Splendid." Reverend Countee's belly rumbled as he chuckled. "When can you start?"

Since I wanted my column in the *Living Way* to be separate and distinct from the one in the *Evening Star*, I wrote for the *Living Way* under the pseudonym "Iola." I thought it had a nice ring to it. Every week I sent a letter to the publication while also fulfilling my editorial duties with the other paper.

It was a lot to take on.

Sometimes I found myself working into the wee hours of the morning, perfecting my sentence structure, making sure that the material was readable and approachable. I was stretched thin. I didn't have much left to give my class in school.

The din of classroom chatter was loud enough to make my head ache. My class numbered nearly fifty students, and they were not as engaged as previous classes. I rapped my knuckles against my desk.

"All right, quiet now," I said. But the students continued their chitchat.

I rubbed my forehead with my hand. I really did have a headache. I longed to be in my room back at the boarding house, at my desk where I could write. Instead, I was warring with grade-school children.

Iola was a success. My words spread like wildfire across the state. More papers started picking up my articles for publication. Soon, almost everyone knew about the Iola advice column.

But as successful as I was at my emerging career as a writer, I was not as successful in making teaching a dream job.

There was a knock on the door.

"Ma'am, there is a gentleman asking after you?"

"Did he say who he was?"

"No, but he said he came to meet the famous Iola. Should I tell him to come back after the school day is over?"

"No, I'll take it." I scooted out from behind my desk. I gave my rowdy classroom one last fleeting look and stepped through the door. Iola business was infinitely more interesting than teaching.

Chapter 13

IN CANDLELIGHT, THE WALLS OF THE *EVENING Star* office looked like they were closing in on me. Shadows danced against the dark wood walls, shifting them closer. The printing press keys clanked from the other side of the room.

"That's it for me," Mr. Browne said as he unrolled his sleeves. "Would you like me to walk you home?"

"That's very kind of you, but I do have to finish this." I smiled through my headache.

"Well, I can stay and help you."

"Something tells me you'd be anything but help."

"Some may think we've broken the rules of impropriety. Being alone here at night," said Mr. Browne.

I snorted. "Please. I am no stranger to idle gossip. I don't care a jot what people think of me."

"Sure you do. Or else you wouldn't buy such pretty dresses and ladylike hats," he said with a smile.

"Are you cataloging my wardrobe, Mr. Browne?" I smirked.

I did like flirting with him. He had a rakish quality that he didn't even try to hide. Most gentlemen operated under a thin veneer of gentility. But he put it out there for all to see. I liked the honesty of that.

"I admire finery when I see it." His eyes glowed in the candlelight. Like the shadows on the wall, they closed in on me, enveloping me in a cloud. He coughed to clear his throat, pulling me back to the present. "Come have a late supper with me."

But all I wanted was to flirt, of course—nothing more. I had work to do.

"Goodnight, Mr. Browne."

Mr. Browne shut the front door behind him. I followed closely behind him and locked the door when he left. A young woman at night could never be too careful, even if she was in a respectable part of town. In Memphis, the seedy underbelly of the city was never far. In a few blocks it could transform into a different kind of crowd, especially in these late hours.

Our conversation had buoyed my mood. It was easier to complete my work when I felt like the butterfly schoolgirl I used to be—flirtatious and fun and lighthearted.

All that was left to do was fit the advertisements into the spaces between the columns. Then I would leave the setup at my desk for the typesetting team to review in the morning. From there, they would set the printing keys and print the paper.

One of the advertisements caught my eye:

The People's Grocery: Purveyor of Fancy Groceries and Fine Goods, T. Moss, Calvin McDowell, Will Stewart & Co.

I knew a Thomas Moss here in Memphis. He was a local letter carrier who delivered letters and parcels to the *Free Speech* office. I wondered if this could be the same person. There was only one way to find out. I'd have to go and see for myself.

The People's Grocery was located in a neighborhood called the Curve, a nexus of activity on the edge of Black Memphis.

"Well, if it isn't Miss Ida Wells."

"Tommie Moss, it's good to see you," I said as I planted my hands on my hips and looked upward at the brick store-front and the sign above the door. "This is a fine store."

"Thank you. But I shouldn't take all the credit. I opened it with Calvin McDowell and Will Stewart and some other folks." Tommie's eyes wandered over to a group of boys who were playing a game against the sidewalk.

"Do they usually play here?" I asked, following his gaze and looking at the young boys playing dice. Both white and Black, it was an odd scene.

"Oh, they're all right. They usually clear out after the sheriff makes his rounds and disperses them. You're lucky you caught me here early. That's when I usually come here. In the evenings I'm home with my family."

"Please send Betty my warm regards." I smiled, remembering the friendship I'd developed with Tommie's wife. They were such a loving and strong family. In many ways, they reminded me of my parents.

"My wife would love to see you again. She reads almost every single one of your articles, so I'm sure she'll talk your ear off about your latest publications."

"It is so flattering to count her among my readership. I look forward to speaking with her soon."

"We are both so proud of you. You've done well for yourself." Tommie raised his eyebrows. "A real live female journalist."

"Yes." I smiled politely, even though I did not like being commended on being a female writer. I wanted to be recognized for my accomplishments just as a writer, same as any man.

"Don't stir up too much trouble." He wagged his finger at me.

"I only write the truth."

"Yes, but the people who hold power in this town don't take too kindly to having the lens of truth trained on them. The Masons especially."

"Are you warning me against writing about them?"

Tommie shook his head with a wary smile. "Oh what's the point? I know you're going to blaze your own way. Just like you always do."

"You do know me." I hesitated, wanting to clasp his hand.

He was one of the few people I'd met who reminded me of *home*. It revived something in me. But since we were on the street, and I didn't want to be accused of impropriety, I folded my hands in front of me, remaining an appropriate distance away from Tommie, who was a married man.

"Dinner next week?" he asked.

"I can't next week. I am attending a conference in Kansas and then going on to California."

"Listen to you!"

"Yes, but I haven't traveled much beyond the surrounding areas. It does sound rather grand, but I promise I'm still the same Ida from little old Holly Springs. My aunt lives southeast of San Francisco now. And she has my sisters with her. I will visit them when I am there."

"Uh-oh, will we lose you to California?"

"If it were up to my aunt, I would have moved there yesterday. But no danger of that." I nodded resolutely. I had worked hard to establish my foothold in Memphis society and to establish my voice as a journalist. As much as I missed my sisters, this was where my opportunities were. I wasn't going to throw that overboard just to please my aunt. "No, I am quite determined to stay here in Memphis."

"And we are the better for it. Do write us when you get back into town. And send my regards to your family."

And then Tommie hoisted up a crate from outside the grocery store and carried it inside.

Chapter 14

A TOAST TO IOLA, THE PRINCESS OF THE Press," Aunt Fanny said as she raised her glass of water at the table.

"Please, you'll make me blush." I laughed while I raised my glass to meet hers. We clinked and took a sip.

"You love the compliments; I know you." Annie smirked from the other side of the table.

Gosh, she looked so much like my mother; it made my heart skip when I looked at her. And she'd grown taller, definitely surpassing me. I was under five feet tall, but she was more statuesque. "You look more and more like Mother every day."

"I can hardly remember what she looked like these days. I was so young when she died," Annie said.

"Well, if you ever have any doubt, look in the mirror. Because that's better than any picture I could give you."

"So you prevailed against the railroad?" Aunt Fanny asked.

As I predicted, the lawsuit against the railroad after I was thrown from the train was a long ordeal.

"Yes, and it was a dreadful headline." It was seared in my mind.

A DARKY DAMSEL OBTAINS A VERDICT FOR DAMAGES AGAINST THE CHESAPEAKE & OHIO RAILROAD—WHAT IT COST TO PUT A COLORED SCHOOL TEACHER IN A SMOKING CAR—VERDICT FOR $500

"But it was a handsome reward of five hundred dollars," I said. I had indeed paid for the first-class ticket, it was determined. I was a schoolteacher, which also gave me standing in their eyes.

"Ida, that is a great deal of money." My aunt clutched her chest, her eyes widening. "With that kind of money, you don't need to teach anymore. And don't say you like teaching. I know you don't."

"I won't lie at your table. Teaching has always been a means to an end. But the railroad is appealing the case, and my lawyer says I should be ready for the verdict to be overturned. So I'm keeping some of the money in reserve."

"Ida, may I suggest something?"

"I know what you are going to suggest." I sighed, putting my fork down. I didn't want this pleasant evening to turn into an argument about whether or not I should move to California.

"Then let me try," Annie said, cutting in. "We could be a family again."

"You're having my little sister work on me?" I raised an eyebrow at my aunt. "You yourself admitted that the society was quite limited here."

"The colored community is a great deal smaller than what we're used to—that is true."

"Then why do you think I would live here?" I was a young woman and I wanted to live where there were opportunities to form community. And Memphis held that possibility. "I have worked so hard to make a name for myself in Memphis."

"But now you've made a name for yourself *nationally*. You're traveling the country. Maybe eventually you'll travel the world." Annie scooted closer to me, her pleading eyes searching mine. "The sky is the limit for you."

"Thanks, Annie," I said, reaching out to touch her arm. "You know flattery will get you everywhere with me."

"Nothing is waiting for you back in Memphis. And there is a world of possibility here. And the community needs you."

"Sell your ticket," Aunt Fanny said. "Yes, you should sell your ticket and teach at the local school here until you figure out your next move."

"You really need me here?" I looked at their hopeful faces. It had been a long time since I'd had a sense of family. Besides sending them money every month and the occasional letter, I was largely on my own. My family had scattered to the winds.

Now I had the opportunity to recreate a nuclear family.

I wanted that. I nodded. "All right, I'll stay."

I desperately wanted to believe this was the right move.

I instantly regretted my decision to stay. After my fourth day of teaching in the local school in California, I hurried home in a huff.

"How was your day?" Aunt Fanny asked, sounding hopeful. "Better than yesterday?"

"It was not great." I folded my arms. "For one, the schools here are still segregated."

"The schools are segregated in Memphis, too. I don't see what the problem is."

"But it's different here. The Black community *chose* to have different facilities," I said.

"We are more equipped to prepare our children for a world that will not be kind to them," countered Aunt Fanny.

"Have you actually seen the facilities? They are subpar compared to the other school. It's nonsense to choose that. I've made a mistake."

"What are you saying?" Aunt Fanny asked, alarmed.

"I cannot stay here. I've decided to go back to Memphis. I can't stay here just to please you. I have to live my life."

"But you've already accepted the job. You haven't even worked a full week. Ida, do not do this. If you leave, then you'll have to take your sisters with you. Both girls are an awful lot for you to handle."

"I've written to Mr. Church in Memphis, and he sent me

a check for the amount I need to travel. Annie, come on and get your things. I'll pack for Lily."

If I wanted to keep my family together, I would. But we were not staying in California.

"I'm not going." Annie stubbornly stamped her foot. She may have looked like a young woman, but she still had the childish impulse to throw a tantrum. When I tried to tug at her sleeve, she stepped away from me, moving closer to my aunt. "I'm staying here."

"You cannot stay here. Your aunt says I must take you both."

Annie threw her arms around Aunt Fanny, who hugged her tight.

"I'll let the girl make her own decision," Aunt Fanny said, relenting.

"Well, Annie, is this really what you want?" I frowned at her, remembering her words from only a few days ago. "I thought you wanted to be a family again."

"But," she said, bowing her head low so that she could avoid my pleading eyes, "me and Aunt Fanny's daughter are close in age, and we are the best of friends. And I've made other friends here. And I like it here."

I bit my lip and threw my hands over my head. But I honestly could see her point. My aunt Fanny could provide her with something I could not: stability. Here, Annie had our aunt, a cousin who was her companion, and a roof over her head.

In short, she had the childhood I *wished* I had.

I planted my hands on my hips. "Promise me you'll care for her as if she were your own," I said to Aunt Fanny.

"Of course I will. She's like a daughter to me."

"Then, Annie, you may stay." I sniffled, my heart tight, and then looked over my shoulder at Lily. "Go on and get packed."

"When do we leave?" Lily sniffled into her sleeve. I could tell that she didn't want to be separated from our sister, but she didn't have a choice in the matter. This was Aunt Fanny's line in the sand. And I would honor it.

"We leave tonight."

Chapter 15

THAT MONTH, I BURNED MANY BRIDGES. THE school in Visalia, California, was angry with me for not fulfilling my obligations to them. And then a short stint in Kansas ended sourly. By the time I got back to Memphis and resumed teaching there, I had worked at three different schools in three different states all in the same month. I just wanted a return to normal life.

But that was only a dream.

My editor at the *Free Speech*, my new writing home, narrowed his eyes as he scanned over my article. Reverend Nightingale shifted in his seat and leaned forward, his eyes growing tighter and tighter. His eyes stopped scanning. He looked over the rim of his glasses with a stern look. "Are you sure about this?"

"Yes, sir. I'm sure."

"I don't think this is a good way to endear yourself to your employer."

"I am not here to kowtow to the school board. I write the truth, and this is something that needs to come into the light."

"Blaming the school board for having immoral affairs. I won't sign on to this one. I cannot take the heat right now. You'll have to sign your name on this one."

"If I must."

"First, it was the ministers. Then, it was the Masons and other secret societies and your assertion that they don't really add anything for the community. And now you accuse one of your fellow teachers of having an illicit affair with a white school board member. You might be one of the most controversial journalists in the whole country."

"When you took me on, you hired me to write the stories that affect our communities. There is a lot of white supremacy out there, but that doesn't mean we don't have issues *inside* of our community."

"I know, I know. And we appreciate your contributions. I just worry about you, that's all. If you lose your job . . ." His voice trailed off as he considered the possibilities.

If I lost my job, I would be in a real kettle of fish.

"Maybe it's time to discuss me coming on full-time. Maybe as a part owner of the paper."

"Ida, every paper in the country is clamoring to have you write for them. We'd love to have more of you in these pages.

But before you look into making a big purchase, you might like to look at this."

He passed a piece of paper to me across the table. It was a letter from my lawyer. As I read, my body felt hotter and hotter.

"What? My railroad settlement has been overturned. I knew that it was a possibility, but I didn't think it would be with prejudice."

"So not only do you have to pay back your settlement fee, you'll also have to pay for lawyer's fees," said Reverend Nightingale.

"Sometimes you can be right but still lose, you understand me?" he continued. "Pick your battles. Fight the ones you absolutely gotta fight. Otherwise, you're in the ring swinging at anyone who comes near you. That's not the way to live. I'm not telling you this as your editor. I'm telling you this as a friend."

"But how will I know what I *absolutely* have to fight?"

"You'll know." He nodded grimly. "Trust me, you'll know."

I traveled to Natchez, Mississippi, on newspaper business. Tasked with selling subscriptions to the *Free Speech* and expanding our readership, I was determined to gather as many new customers as possible. My friend Fannie joined me for moral support.

We attended a church function, which had the benefit of having most of the local Black community in the same place.

"Hmm, let's sit over there." Fannie chewed on the inside of her lip as she scoured the pews for a place to sit. I was a general favorite among our readers. But for every admirer I had, I had an enemy. Some of the attendees glared at us when we attempted to sit next to them. I was not welcomed by some of my peers.

"Perhaps you shouldn't have gone after the school board." Fannie smiled uncomfortably as she searched for another pair of seats.

"You sound just like my editor."

"Oh, let's just sit in the back. That should be a safe place for us."

After the meeting we left the building.

"Oh, look! They have roasted nuts." Fannie pointed. "Do you want to go buy some?"

"No thanks," I grumbled under my breath, resenting the current state of my finances. Between paying back the verdict and supporting my family, I was yet again strapped for cash.

A reporter came up to me and asked me, "Do you care to comment on the recent lynching in your hometown of Memphis?"

"What lynching?" I frowned.

"What I have here is that three men were murdered in cold blood in a field for some scuffle that took place at the Curve."

My heart started to beat faster.

"The Curve?" Fannie covered her mouth with her hand.

She knew the place well. We all did. It was a prominent part of the community.

"I know it well." I nodded solemnly. My breath hitched. A dear friend of mine worked at the Curve. And I hoped to God he wasn't involved.

"Who were they?"

"Thomas Moss, Calvin McDowell, and Will Stewart."

My knees buckled and I steadied myself on Fannie.

I knew them well.

Chapter 16

I CLUTCHED MY PURSE CLOSE TO MY CHEST AS I hurried down the street. As soon as I'd returned to Memphis, I bought a gun, which I'd quickly stowed in my handbag. I had contraband. I was not supposed to arm myself, but the alternative was to be cornered by the mob without any means of protection.

"Did you have any difficulty getting here?" Betty Moss asked as she ushered me inside her home. She rubbed her belly, which was already showing her pregnancy. Tommie would never get a chance to see his second child.

"No, the streets were empty." I smiled tightly. This neighborhood was usually bustling with activity. But the streets were eerily quiet since I'd returned home. Black residents were being arrested left and right, accused of being conspirators of the People's Grocery rioters. The white people accused the Black owners of People's Grocery of taking business away from them. An angry mob came after them, killing Tommie, Calvin McDowell, and Will Stewart.

Of course, this was a fallacy. The owners had done nothing wrong. Their only crime was being Black and prosperous.

"They rounded dozens of people up. People are afraid that they'll start arresting folks again, even after the . . . lynching. I even bought a pistol," I said.

"But they banned it. Every single Black person in the city who wants to buy a gun can't. By court order, mind you. What's more is that a judge has given the mob permission to shoot any of us if they suspect we'll cause any trouble," Betty said. I felt sick. We could be shot with permission from the court just because a white person suspected something.

"It's insanity. I feel like we're all sitting ducks here." I took a cautious step forward, approaching Betty as gently as possible. She had been through hell, and what I was about to ask her was great indeed. "I've heard so many stories about what happened that night. You don't have to talk about it if you don't want to."

"I'd rather speak about it than have even more lies spread about that fateful day," Betty said.

"What happened?"

"Apparently, some of the neighborhood kids were playing marbles," Betty said. Her eyes were hooded from crying and not sleeping. She gestured to the teakettle. "Would you like some tea?"

"Yes, thank you." I nodded politely even though I had no desire for tea. In fact, I'd had little appetite for anything since I'd heard the news of Tommie's murder.

"A fight broke out and then it escalated," Betty said. "There was talk of the white shopkeepers assembling a posse. So the men who owned the People's Grocery responded in kind."

"As any sane person would do," I said.

"They had men posted inside the store at night, in case any trouble came. And of course trouble came."

"But was Thomas there?"

"Yes, he was there, but he was in the back, looking over the account books. When he heard shots fired, he left the store. Her voice quivered. Then she buried her head in her hands. "He was here, at home, when they arrested him."

"And then a mob came and broke them out of jail," I prompted her gently.

"That's what the paper said." Her gaze strayed to the newspaper on the table. Her eyes narrowed, and an angry tear escaped and trickled down her cheek. "You know that was published the next day? The very next day?" She pushed the paper toward me.

RIDDLED. The mob's summary
execution of three negro prisoners.
Taken to an old field and filled with shot.
Finding of Moss, McDowell, and
Stewart's bodies.

"If it was published the day after the . . . lynching, that means that whoever wrote this article was probably at the lynching." I swallowed hard. I still could not face that word head-on, especially when it involved one of my closest friends.

"Of course he was there. They were *all* there. Even the judge himself is responsible. Judge DuBose promised to gather a posse together and to silence the rowdy Blacks," Betty said, her fists tightening.

"They cannot get away with this," I said.

"White people can get away with anything." She slammed her fist on the table. "Even murder."

There was a moment of silence as both our minds raced.

"I'll never let them hear the end of this," I said as I shot up from my seat and paced in front of the fireplace. "Until we have justice, there will be no peace on this issue."

"People are finished with this place," said Betty. "Tom's dying words were for people to move west, because there is no justice for us in this city."

"And I suppose that is what you'll do," I said.

"I will follow the instructions of my husband. And you would do best to do the same."

"I can't leave." I folded my arms, erecting my wall of stubbornness. My aunt was the last person to urge me to move west, and that ended horribly for me. I wasn't going to make the same mistake twice. "I still have work to do here at the paper, demanding justice for this heinous crime."

"Then all I can do is beg you to be careful. Remember,

that mob can be reassembled at any time. The white people are scared," Betty said.

"They're scared when we're the ones being murdered?" I howled. "It's too unbelievable."

"Believe it," said Betty. "And best believe that if you stir up too much trouble, they'll come for you too."

It was not in my nature to sit idly by and watch the chariots of justice pass over our community. Betty Moss was right to warn me against retribution, but I figured I was right in following my gut instinct. And my gut instinct told me to hold the perpetrators accountable.

A fire simmered in my veins.

I wrote a scathing article about the lynching at the Curve. The article spread like wildfire, with numerous papers across the country reprinting my fierce critique on white lies and mob justice.

And it attracted local attention, too, when they visited me at the paper.

The superintendent of the City Railway Company twiddled his thumbs as he looked around the small *Free Speech* office. His companion, the treasurer of the railway, looked out the windows at the few people on Beale Street. Although our numbers in Memphis were steadily dwindling, Black people still had a sizable presence here.

"I'm sorry?" I raised my eyebrows, surprised by what the superintendent was saying. "Can you say that again?"

"We were just saying that we were curious as to why our ridership has dwindled."

"It's a wonder, isn't it," I said. "Black people are leaving this city in droves. Why do *you* think your ridership has declined?"

"Well, we've noticed it's come primarily from the colored population," the superintendent said.

"On account of you people being afraid of electricity," the treasurer added.

My eyes narrowed. "I don't think this has anything to do with your change from horse-drawn compartments to electrical ones." I folded my arms, feeling my blood boiling. "Besides, the change to electric happened six months ago."

"We want to assure people that it is perfectly safe to travel in the cars," said the superintendent.

"And that any discourteous incidents that happen to you all will be dealt with swiftly and severely," added the treasurer.

"We'd appreciate it if you relay this to your community," said the superintendent.

"I don't know if I can advise my people to go against what their conscience dictates," I said. I knew this had nothing to do with the change to electric cars.

"We just don't understand it. Sales have dropped off quite a bit."

"And how long have you noticed the decline?" I asked.

"I'd say it's been about six weeks," said the treasurer.

"I suspect it might have something to do with the lynching that happened six weeks ago," I said.

"Well, I don't know. . . ." His voice trailed up. He was clearly uncomfortable with where the conversation was headed.

Good. I wanted him to feel uncomfortable. I wanted everyone in this city to be discomfited and disturbed by the lynching of the owners of the People's Grocery.

"We had nothing to do with that lynching!" said the superintendent. "We're owned by a bunch of Northerners, for goodness' sake. Find the men who are guilty. But to punish us . . ."

"I have no way of knowing who exactly was present at the lynching. But I find white people complicit in this crime."

"But, ma'am . . ."

"There was chatter for days leading up to the lynch mob's crimes. There was open plotting to cause damage to the People's Grocery. And no one did anything about it," I said calmly, even though I could feel the heat rising in me.

"I can assure you . . ."

"We gave Black men good work when we laid the tracks for the new electric line. It's only right that they show their gratitude by patronizing the railway," said the treasurer.

Huh. I looked back and forth at them. These men obviously could not comprehend what had happened in this city. They couldn't comprehend something larger than lining their pockets with money from the Black community.

"Now, if you will excuse me, gentlemen, I have an article to write." I crossed the office in a few long strides and swung open the door. "As a matter of fact, this one is about encouraging more Black citizens to head west. And to save their pennies in order to do so. And one of the easiest ways to save money is to walk rather than pay streetcar fare."

I smiled politely, then ushered them out.

Then I crossed the room, deep in thought. The *Free Speech* business manager, Mr. Fleming, chuckled when he looked at my furrowed brow.

"There she goes again. I know when she's itching to get a pen in her hands."

"Of course I'm going to write up this conversation. It's a perfect example of white indifference to Black Memphis." When I reached my notebook, I sat down and scribbled furiously.

"I ought to be worried that you're encouraging our principal subscribers to leave town," said Mr. Fleming.

"But you know you shouldn't worry, right? I have been selling subscriptions up and down the railroads any chance I can get. Our subscriber list spans an area outside Memphis."

"We are finally in the black and making a profit. So tread carefully, okay?" Mr. Fleming's eyebrows upturned. He winced when he said this, probably aware that I didn't take too kindly to following orders.

"It is odd though. We are encouraging people to follow Moss's advice and head west. But then we're leaving the South firmly in the hands of the white supremacists. They could shut out Black people from participating in the political process for a century," I said.

"Very possible. But we should follow our own advice."

"And leave Memphis?" I asked, feeling my wall of stubbornness erecting at the thought of being forced out. But defiance lasted only a minute and reason got the better of me. I slouched in defeat at the thought. "I suppose we should. But where would we go?"

"Let's give it some thought. Meanwhile, do you have a story to file?"

Chapter 17

THE MISSISSIPPI RIVER WAS HIGH AND WIDE this time of year. The rains had made it swell, so I stood along the bluffs with dozens of other onlookers who came to see a large group of migrants starting their journey to Oklahoma.

There must have been hundreds of them making the journey. Too poor to afford the train fare to the Oklahoma territories, this group of migrants did what they could with what they had—converting wagons into transport vessels with no cover and shelter from the sun. The men walked alongside with what they could carry, and the women and children rode along in the wagons. It was like something out of one of my many books—like the pioneer settlers venturing into the West with covered wagons.

I waved my hands to them, most of them strangers to me,

hitched up in wagons with all the possessions they could carry for their journey ahead. I didn't know most of them personally, yet I felt a kinship to them.

J. L. Fleming from the newspaper stood next to me, waving at the people also boarding boats. He looked uneasily to the bluffs far away from us, where a gaggle of white observers watched in strained silence. "Look at them, just standing silent over there."

"I can almost see the heat rippling off their shoulders. It helps that we're here in large numbers. It makes it difficult for them to single one or two of us out."

"I suppose we should keep waving and smiling." There were hundreds leaving Memphis, bound for the Oklahoma Territory. Eventually thousands would leave, their jaws clenched tightly, gazing to the other side of the river with a determination born of self-preservation. A better, more just life was hopefully on the other side of the river. Like Tommie Moss said, there was no justice left for us in Memphis.

"Well, what is it they want?" asked Mr. Fleming crossly, looking at the white people lining the banks, watching what was happening. "They clearly despise our presence here. Yet they're angry that we're leaving."

"They just want us to be subservient and buy their goods and ride their streetcars and keep our mouths shut," I said.

"They don't know what they want. And that's what makes them dangerous. We have to decide on our own wants and needs and find a place that will allow us to pursue them."

A man walked down the dock and jumped into one of the boats. His yellow dog, spooked at the sight of the gangplank, trotted back and paced nervously as he looked to the man. His owner called to him.

"Come here. If you stay here, they might lynch you too!"

The bluffs erupted in laughter, myself included. We managed to find humor in the moment, but there was truth in the jest. I looked to the white men on the far bluffs, who were definitely not laughing at the man's joke.

In truth, it was no laughing matter. The rage was nearly palpable, and I was aware of the fact that they could reassemble the mob in a heartbeat. These angry men were the mob.

One of the ferries was unloading on the other side of the river, so far away I couldn't make out the passengers disembarking on the Arkansas side. But I sent them a silent prayer all the same.

Dust that Memphis dirt off your boots and never come back. Be safe and flourish.

"We should be going." I gave one more nervous look at the white men and turned to leave.

"The river swells this time of year. The lowlands might be flooded, and then they'll be trapped," Mr. Fleming said. "The only way to travel then would be by train."

"But these are the people who can't afford the train. If that happens, we'll send a collection plate to all the churches and raise funds to help them," I said.

"I saw at least two women who looked like they were

going to give birth. Surely they should stay and be in confinement."

"Women are stronger than men give them credit for. They're just as determined as any man to leave this place behind," I said.

"And what about you, Miss Ida? Will you leave this place behind? Will you leave little old me behind?"

"Eventually, yes. We have already decided that we can't run the paper out of Memphis for much longer. So I suspect soon we'll be printing from another location." I walked on slowly for a bit before speaking. "I am visiting the Oklahoma Territory."

"Don't you ever think about settling down?" Mr. Fleming asked. "Maybe with someone nice like me?"

I shook my head vigorously. I certainly had no plans of marrying *him*. But I thought longer about the general notion of getting married and settling down, perhaps having a child or two. Most women swooned at the thought of being a wife. But I wasn't like most women. The idea of being a wife didn't excite me. Neither did the idea of motherhood.

"No." I shook my head. "I'm just getting started."

Beyond the Mississippi Delta and the plains of Arkansas was Oklahoma Territory. Using my railroad pass, I traversed the territory in search of information for my people back in Memphis—everywhere from Oklahoma City to Guthrie and in between. I had long advised them to move west and seek out newly opened government land, but I didn't know the logistics of doing so. And since I was a thorough journalist who wanted to be relied on, I went in search of the facts. Before they set off, I wanted them to know what they might be facing.

When I returned home from my three-week journey, I was bedraggled. I collapsed onto my bed and felt the comfort of being back at home in Memphis. My sister Lily, who lived with a woman who was teaching her how to cook, had come to spend the night with me so that she could hear about my travels.

"Tell me everything about your trip," she said.

"I will in a moment," I said, my eyes still closed. I was so tired, but I knew Lily was lonely without me.

"Is it really as true as they say?" Lily asked. "Can you really buy land for nickels and pennies?"

"Where did you hear that from?"

"Lots of folks are talking about it," Lily said.

"Well, it's not that cheap, but it is certainly a great deal cheaper than land is here in Memphis." I propped myself onto my elbow so that I could see her better. A smirk tugged at my lips as I said, "I was there when they opened up the government land to the new settlers. There was quite a rush."

I remembered the mash of people clambering to buy land from the government outpost. It was quite a scene to behold: all those hopeful, determined people settling into an unknown land that belonged mostly to Native Americans.

"It seems like you almost envy them."

"I must admit that the prices are attractive. Even we could own property out there." I lay back and looked at the ceiling, trying to envision the possibility. "We could set up the *Free Press* there. A good deal of our subscribers are already situated there, and they expressed a wish to have the paper nearby. And between covering the new settlements and dealings with the local tribes and dealing, of course, with the white people there, there would be no shortage of stories."

"Hmm," Lily huffed beside me, then fell silent. After a while she spoke. "I hope you stay closer to a more established city. I think that's the only way you'd be happy."

"Why do you say that?" I asked.

"Well, you got out of Holly Springs quick as you could. And you took to Memphis like a natural. You didn't want to stay in Visalia with Aunt Fanny and Annie because of the limited Black community and limited society. I just think you need to be in the thick of it all."

"Perhaps you're right." I was impressed by her powers of deduction and her keen observations. My littlest sister was growing up before my very eyes. With her grown, that would make all of my siblings adults now. I had fulfilled my obligation to my parents and raised everyone to adulthood. Sure, I mainly helped most of them financially, but they didn't need me in the way they needed me when they were younger. I had discharged my duties as the oldest sister.

I gave myself an inner pat on the back.

"Next week I'm off to Philadelphia and then to visit T. Thomas Fortune's newspaper in New York City. He's a well-regarded editor, if you don't know. Maybe I'll check out the opportunities on the East Coast," I said.

"It seems like nonsense for you to be leaving. You've only just returned!" Lily exclaimed. She looked bashfully to her lap. "Oh, please, let me come with you."

"Not a chance." I sat up and faced her. "Even though we're on the heels of summer, this isn't a vacation. This is for work."

"I want to see New York just the same as you do. Besides, it is not safe here anymore. Not after all the trouble you've stirred up at the *Free Speech*," she said.

"You should be blaming the lynch mob, not *me*." I crossed my arms and scowled at her, feeling righteous indignation ripple through my bones. But she hadn't been touched by the hardness of life as I had. I still needed to take care of her. I briefly considered loaning her my pistol that I'd purchased right after the lynching. But Lily didn't know how to handle a gun. I sighed into my pillow. "I will make sure you are well looked after. As I have always done."

Then I rolled over to face away from her. Without even bothering to change into my night clothes, I drifted into a restless sleep.

Chapter 18

BECAUSE OF MY TRIP TO OKLAHOMA AND my short stint at home, I arrived at the conference in Philadelphia two weeks after it started. I'd apparently missed all the best speakers, because the sessions I attended were nothing of note. Before I had even settled in, the conference was over, and I quickly hurried to my train.

Mrs. Fanny Coppin, a famed teacher and the wife of Reverend Levi Coppin, was kind enough to accompany me to the train station. "You have everything you need?"

"Yes, thank you so much for your hospitality, and for showing me your school today."

"Certainly! What a treat to have the famous Ida B. Wells at my school. We'll be talking about it for ages, I dare say."

"I started out a teacher. I learned quite a bit during my years in the classroom," I said.

"And look at you now. I mean really look at what you've accomplished. You are treading where no other Black woman has ever gone before. You're an editor and a writer, mentioned in the same class as Frederick Douglass and the like."

"It is hard to wrap my head around," I admitted. "Honestly, this whole city of Philadelphia is hard to wrap my head around. It is so vast and storied. And the Black ladies we met with the other day—such finery the likes of which most people have never seen before."

"Yes, we have done well up here in the North. It's not without its complications from the white people, but it's certainly not what you are forced to deal with in Memphis." She paused a moment, as if to give a moment of silence for our fallen friends who died in the lynching. Then she cleared her throat and threaded her arm through mine. "As for finery, wait until you see New York."

"New York." I sighed, shaking my head. "I feel a bit overwhelmed just by the thought of it."

"Oh yes, it is quite a grand city. You will find plenty of stories there. Have you made suitable arrangements for when you get to the station in New York?"

"T. Thomas Fortune is picking me up from the train, and then we will head straight to the *New York Age* office," I said.

"Oh, I shall always cherish meeting with you." Her eyes tightened at the poignant lilt in her voice. "You represent the hope of the next generation. I am honored to know you."

She clasped my hands and gripped them warmly, pulling

me toward her a bit, then released me so that I could board the train to New York.

As the train lurched forward, I watched intently as the landscape and buildings changed. I was often pensive on these train journeys. And this time I felt such a weight of responsibility.

Was I the hope of the next generation?

That was an enormous burden to carry. Yet, I felt like I had a role in the race discussions to come. I was not content living in a world where I was treated like a second-class citizen, where I was ripped from train cars or where I had to carry a gun for fear of falling prey to the mob. That world was not one that I accepted.

I demanded America's promise of liberty and justice for all.

My world had gotten so much bigger than when I was a young woman riding a mule to teach in the country schools. Now I was a woman traveling hundreds of miles away, seeing this vast country as a Black woman in America. I could scarcely believe the ability I had to travel for work.

But I had actively made this happen. I did it.

Stepping off the train in Jersey City, I stood taller as I squared my shoulders and held my head up. I was a force to be reckoned with.

Perhaps that's why T. Thomas Fortune, one of the most preeminent Black journalists in the country, made it a point to meet me at the station. He was familiar with my writing, and while we admired each other, we didn't always agree on things. Still, a man of his stature meeting me on the platform reminded me just how many people were familiar with my work.

"Thank you for taking time out of your busy schedule just to fetch me," I said.

"Of course. We are honored to have the Princess of the Press herself."

"Stop with that," I said with a grin.

"Well, I've spent a long time trying to convince you to come here and consider hanging your hat in New York. And it seems like now you are here, you'll have to stay."

"Why is that?"

"You haven't read the morning papers, have you?" He tilted his head to the side, frowning slightly.

"No, I was with Mrs. Coppin and Bishop Turner all day, and then we went straight to the station. What is it? What's happened?"

"I brought one of the papers with me so that you could see for yourself," said Mr. Fortune. He looked into my eyes and handed me the paper. I read the headline.

FREE SPEECH DESTROYED. IDA B. WELLS EXILED FROM THE CITY.

I couldn't believe what I was reading. They destroyed the *Free Speech*?

"The office was burned down," said Mr. Fortune. "Destroyed by a mob. You can't go back."

I still wasn't processing everything.

"Exiled? They're not going to let me come back to Memphis?" I cried.

"It seems so. And judging by what you've been reporting on the past few months, I don't think that's an empty threat."

My eyes glazed over as I thought of the white men on the bluffs of the Mississippi River, standing in silent rage as they watched hundreds of Black residents wriggle free from their clutches. I'd felt they were almost at a boiling point, and it seems I was right. They had reassembled their mob, stormed the *Free Speech*, and destroyed everything in the office.

I thought of my business partner, who warned me to tamp down my reporting of the lynching. Had Fleming been there when the mob attacked? My breath hitched as I remembered the warning Betty Moss gave to me after her husband was lynched by a mob.

Best believe that if you stir up too much trouble, they'll come for you too.

And where was my sister Lily in all this? She bore the same family name as me. If the mob was out for vengeance against me, they might go after her instead. I hastily folded the paper and turned my frenzied gaze to Mr. Fortune.

"I need to send a telegram. Straightaway!"

My breakfast plate stared back at me, cool and unappetizing. I was feeling anxious and depressed a few days after the news of my paper being destroyed. The depression filled my belly with regret and fear, so much so that I had no room for food. I wasn't hungry. I hadn't been for days.

The front door to Mr. Fortune's house opened, and I jumped from the noise. I really was on edge, eager to hear word from my people in Memphis. But it was only Mr. Fortune's business partner, Mr. John H. Harmon. He took off his hat and held it over his chest.

"Good morning." He bowed politely. "Any news yet?"

I shook my head slightly. It was all I could muster.

"I really wish you would eat something, Miss Wells." Mrs. Fortune reached across the table to grab my hand but stopped short. "It would do you some good to get some food in you."

"Thank you. Perhaps I will in a bit." I smiled tightly, not wanting to be rude. But I couldn't think of food at a time like this.

"Well, if you're finished breaking fast, we were wondering if we might speak with you." Mr. Fortune got up from the table and gestured to the hallway.

We walked to his study across the hall.

"We were wondering if you were considering settling into New York. More permanently."

"I don't know where I am going to live. Every dollar I had was tied up in the *Free Speech*. Now that it is gone and now that I am exiled from my own city, I find myself quite unmoored."

"Would you consider anchoring yourself here in the city and working at the *New York Age*?" Mr. Peterson asked.

"That is kind," I said, wanting to be grateful. While the

offer was generous, I was not sure I was interested. I had been the editor and co-owner of my own newspaper. I didn't want a demotion to mere writer. "Very charitable of you," I said.

New York was expansive and expensive. I would need a great deal of money to support myself here.

"We would of course compensate you." Mr. Harmon nodded. He crossed the room and sat down in the armchair opposite me. "Should you accept, you would be a salaried writer. And, if you are amenable, we would offer you a twenty-five percent stake in the *New York Age* in exchange for your *Free Press* subscription list."

"So I would be a co-owner with you?" I asked Mr. Fortune.

"That is right."

"Pardon me, sir. But there is a telegram for Miss Ida." The maid curtsied. "And a letter."

"By all means, please bring it here," Mr. Fortune said. He waved his hand toward me, beckoning the maid to hand off the letters with haste.

"It's from my lawyer, B. F. Booth." I scanned the dispatch quickly, breathing a sigh of relief when I reached its end. "He says that Fleming made it out of Memphis safely. He left just before the mob ransacked the building."

I ripped open the letter, quickly reading it through.

"And this one is from a neighbor of mine in Memphis. She assures me that my sister is in safe hands. She begs me not to come back, because the white community has vowed to kill me if I set foot back in Memphis. She warns of more blood-shed and begs me to prevent the making of more widows."

Prevent the making of more widows. My stomach flipped and my heart was heavy.

"I am glad both Mr. Fleming and your sister are safe. We will let you have some privacy." Mr. Fortune placed his hands on his knees and lifted himself out of the armchair. His colleague followed him across the room and to the door. He turned back and said, "Please consider my offer."

I paused, still flustered from the plea in the letter.

"I will," I said slowly. "But first I'd like to ask what I am to be permitted to write."

"I'm sorry, I don't understand," he said.

"My business partner, Mr. Fleming, did not like me writing about the lynching in Memphis. He became increasingly frightened, and of course for good reason. The mob was set on us. But I cannot allow angry white men to dictate what I write and the truth that I tell. I guess I'd like to know if you'd like them to dictate the terms of our journalism."

"Certainly not. We print the facts and we disseminate the truth. The truth, Miss Wells. So, it might do well to dispense with the innuendos of your very last article at the *Free Press*."

"You caught that one?" I smiled ruefully. I remembered the last story that I logged with my paper before I traveled to the East Coast. It was an article about how there had been more lynchings in the South since the one in Memphis that killed Tommie Moss. And more than half of them cried false rape. In the article, I suggested that those false allegations were just pretext for killing with impunity. I explained how, where, and why the Black men were lynched:

> Eight negroes lynched since last issue of
> the *Free Speech,* one at Little Rock,
> Ark., last Saturday morning where the
> citizens broke(?) into the penitentiary
> and got their man; three near Anniston,
> Ala., one near New Orleans; and three at
> Clarksville, Ga., the last three for killing
> a white man, and five on the same old
> racket—the new alarm about raping white
> women. The same programme of hanging,
> then shooting bullets into the lifeless bodies
> was carried out to the letter.
>
> Nobody in this section of the country
> believes the old thread-bare lie that Negro
> men rape white women. If Southern white
> men are not careful, they will overreach
> themselves and public sentiment will have a
> reaction; a conclusion will then be reached
> which will be very damaging to the moral
> reputation of their women.

"Ida, that article was picked up by the *Commercial Appeal*, in which one of the editorials called on you to be burned at the stake," said Mr. Fortune. "Yes, I do remember that one. That is probably what did you in."

I bowed my head, looking at my lap. I'd been edgy in my last *Free Speech* article, and I supposed I was supposed to feel guilty for taking a jab at the moral reputation of white womanhood. But I didn't feel an inkling of regret. That article demonstrated what my research had indicated for months— that the rationales for lynching usually fell into one of two categories. Three out of the eight lynchings had been justified because the men were allegedly brutish, and the other five lynchings had occurred because white women were allegedly violated. Rape was a heinous crime that should be taken seriously, but these men were not killed for raping women. I was merely busting that myth. "The *Commercial Appeal* called for me to be burned at the stake like Joan of Arc? I'd like to read a copy of that if you have it."

"I will get a copy for you," he said. "But I do want to say this before I leave: you have shed light on a very serious issue in this country, the lynch law and the chilling effect it has on the Black community. We would expect you to keep the spotlight on that, if you are able."

I felt urgency. And I wanted the chance he was offering me.

"If those are the terms, I accept your offer," I said. "And for my first column, I'd like to do an in-depth look at lynching in America."

Chapter 19

WHEN I HAD ALL MY AFFAIRS IN ORDER and had moved into my own lodgings separate from Mr. Fortune's, I was ready to begin work. My notebooks were splayed across my desk as I extracted names and dates from the chain of events after the owners of the People's Grocery were shot like dogs in that field. But I also looked at the circumstances surrounding the lynchings across the South. The Black community was hurting, and I felt that I could voice our concerns—now louder and more forcefully than I had ever done.

I wanted the country and the world to hear our pleas for justice.

Lynching was on the rise, and there was almost always one of two reasons given. The first reason was that the Black person threatened a white man's life or appeared menacing to him. The second reason was that the Black person (almost always described as a brutish man) had impugned a woman's moral character in some way, had debased her by ogling her, by being alone with her, by spending too much time with her. Even when close proximity between white women and Black men was consensual, white men categorized it as rape.

And with these two justifications, lynch law claimed so many lives. It was swift and severe and barbaric. Men were strung up or shot or disfigured or a combination of the three. Lynching was happening with more frequency than it had in the past and no longer could people turn a blind eye to our plight, no longer could white people claim that lynch mobs were an uncommon but justified occurrence.

Lynching in America was becoming commonplace. That fact terrified me.

The brutality of this injustice kept me awake at night. I couldn't sleep. No one should have been able to justify that savagery.

I scribbled onto the page:

> It is with no pleasure I have dipped my hands in the corruption here exposed. Somebody must show that the Afro-American race is more sinned against than sinning, and it seems to have fallen upon me to do so. The awful death-roll that Judge Lynch is calling every week

is appalling, not only because of the lives
it takes, the rank cruelty and outrage to
the victims, but because of the prejudice
it fosters and the stain it places against the
good name of a weak race.

The Afro-American is not a bestial
race. If this work can contribute in any
way toward proving this, and at the
same time arouse the conscience of the
American people to a demand for justice
to every citizen, and punishment by law
for the lawless, I shall feel I have done my
race a service.

I sat back, smiling as I reread the first couple paragraphs,
feeling quite pleased with the sharpness of my pen. Yes, this
would get the attention of America. I brought the pen to the
page and wrote on and on, burning the midnight oil until I
was satisfied with an initial draft.

It took me weeks to complete my treatise, but when I finally
finished, I brought the thick stack of papers to Mr. Fortune,
eager to publish at least some of it. He surprised me by agree-
ing to publish all of my essay, even though it would take up a
significant portion of the publication's pages.

In a seven-column article in the *New York Age* titled "The
Truth about Lynching," I outlined the false justifications of

lynching in the South. It was a front-page spread that no one could ignore. While we waited for the column to gain traction in the white press, I used my twice-weekly column to continue to speak against the brutality of mob violence.

I waited for white America to wake up. I had laid all the grisly facts at their feet. Other newspapers had ample time to syndicate my columns, to circulate the facts among their own readership. I waited and waited for my fellow Americans to join in my outrage, but they were mostly silent on the issue of lynch law.

A few weeks later, I paced in the *New York Age* office, feeling irritation radiating down my spine. In many ways, I felt more empowered than ever in my new position at the *Age*. Mr. Fortune was not as cautious as my business partners had been at the *Free Speech*. He allowed me to write the bare, unabashed truth in the pages of the *Age* without the usual concessions that blunted the edge of my rebukes.

My articles on the horrors of the South had real teeth meant to start a national dialogue about lynching. So why was no one talking about it?

"You'll wear a hole in the floor if you keep pacing like that." Mr. Fortune smirked from his desk in the corner of our office.

"It helps me think." I stopped pacing and sighed, then turned on my heels to face him. "I need to make my next article more rousing, more confrontational. That will get the ball rolling on legal reforms."

"I don't think you could get more rousing than your June twenty-fifth publication." He sank back in his chair and crossed his arms. "You're being too hard on yourself. You have sparked a conversation in the Black community. You even have a meeting with two women this very hour. They were so roused by your articles that they had to meet with you. They wouldn't take no for an answer."

I shrugged. Mrs. Victoria Earle Matthews and Miss Maritcha Lyons were prominent members of New York and Brooklyn society. Their praise carried a lot of weight. I was grateful for their appreciation of my work, but I failed to see how it would help further the cause of my anti-lynching campaign. In my experience, society women were supportive behind closed doors, but they often lacked the gumption to mount a public campaign. I mumbled under my breath, "Let's see if they can stomach the fight."

In short order, the two women arrived at the *New York Age* office. Mrs. Matthews was the first to enter, followed by Miss Lyons. The petticoats between them filled the front of the office with billowing fabric much finer than anything I owned. But I could tell these two women were not just society ladies. There was a fierce intensity in their eyes as they honed in on me, and I wasn't the only one who noticed. Mr. Fortune blinked rapidly, then shot up from his seat.

"Ladies," he said with a small bow. "It is an honor to have you in our humble office. We are not used to having such esteemed company."

"I rather doubt that. You have the most esteemed woman right here under your roof." Mrs. Matthews nodded politely in my direction. "Miss Ida B. Wells, it is such a pleasure to make your acquaintance. I am Victoria Earle Matthews, and this is Maritcha Lyons."

"Very good to meet you." Miss Lyons beamed from beside her friend.

"Please have a seat," I said with a tight smile, pointing to a pair of chairs across from my desk. I was nervous about entertaining society ladies. Surely they would find me lacking in some ways. But these two women didn't seem to be turned off by the frankness of my writing. Perhaps we had more in common than I'd initially thought.

"I am sure you are quite busy, so we want to get straight to the point." Miss Lyons sat on the edge of her chair. "I have been speaking with my fellow women of Brooklyn."

"And I have been speaking with many women in New York," Mrs. Matthews added. "And we were all so moved by the paper on Southern horrors."

"So much so that we are raising money to allow you to publish your paper again. This time with a wider distribution." Miss Lyons clasped her hands together. "And after your paper has gotten in the hands of more people, we would love to show you our appreciation by hosting a public testimonial."

"Oh, goodness." I blinked in surprise. It was a lot to take in. But I was so flattered, I couldn't help but entertain this extravagant offer. "I was just telling Mr. Fortune that I didn't think the public cared enough about my crusade to spring into motion."

"Then let me put your mind at ease." Miss Lyons's upturned eyebrows pleaded with me. "We have over two hundred women devoted to your cause. Some of them leading ladies of society."

"There is Mrs. Sarah Garnet of New York City." Mrs. Matthews held up her finger, counting along with the names. "And Dr. Susan McKinney from Brooklyn."

"And your influence spreads beyond our sister cities to Boston and Philadelphia." Miss Lyons nodded emphatically. "Mrs. Gertrude Mossell and Mrs. Josephine St. Pierre Ruffin are supporters of your cause, just to name a few."

"So?" Mrs. Matthews leaned forward in her seat, her eyes alight with excitement. "Will you allow us to boost your voice in this way?"

My mouth was agape. This would be a huge endeavor, big enough to catch the attention of the national press. With the reprinting of my article and the involvement of the leading figures of Black society, my anti-lynching campaign was sure to capture the nation's attention. I nodded emphatically along with the ladies sitting across from me.

"Count me in."

Chapter 20

I PEEKED THROUGH THE CURTAIN, OPENING ITS velvet fabric just wide enough to sneak half my face through. The crowd was large. Every seat was filled. There were even some people standing in the back of the auditorium. The din of the theater grew louder as a few of the ladies walked onto the platform.

The finest silks and taffeta and cotton, tailored in dresses designed by the most talented designers, graced the seats of Lyric Hall. I looked down at my dress. It was well-made and fit me perfectly, but fashion was a luxury I splurged on. I spent more money on dresses and hats and fabric than I did on almost anything. But even my good dress was not as fine as the expensive outfits of the leading ladies of New York and Brooklyn.

The ladies of the committee were also able to drum up

interest in Boston and Philadelphia. I recognized some faces from my time in Philadelphia at the AME General Conference. Some of them I recognized not because I'd ever met them but because I'd seen their faces in the society pages. This was such a grand affair.

This had to be the biggest event of its kind.

Never had lynch mobs received so much attention by New York society. New York was famous for its indifference to outsiders, with its closed-off cliques and who's who lists. But they were all here to support my paper and to further the cause of fighting against lynching and brutality against Black people. If my parents could see me now, they would be in awe.

I missed them, more than I had in a long time—as much as I had missed them when I rode the freight train home to Holly Springs, draped in black and smothered with grief.

My eyes welled with tears. It was too much to bear. I stepped away from the curtains, allowing them to shut out the big world that was pressing into me. My chest tightened, and I clutched my collar as an acute wave of panic flooded over me.

God, all these people are here to hear me speak?

Mrs. Matthews bustled in, followed closely by a troop of musicians. She held up her hand, halting them in their tracks. "Just wait here for a moment. There will be introductions and club resolutions to get though before you go on."

Her confident smile faltered when she found me hiding in the corner. I blushed and looked away from her, embarrassed that one of the organizers of this grand event had seen me cowering in fear.

"You all right, dear? You look a little out of sorts." She frowned as she appraised me.

"It's just hot in here, that's all." I straightened my collar, trying to be as convincing as possible. But Mrs. Matthews's perceptive eyes saw through the lie.

"Miss Wells, you're going to be brilliant up there, you'll see." She tilted her head to the side as she rubbed my shoulder in soft circles. The motherly gesture eased my tense muscles a bit. "You have a little while yet. The musicians will play in a few minutes, and then I will get up and introduce you. And then you'll have the floor."

"I will try my best not to disappoint you."

"Nonsense. You'll be fine." She gripped my shoulders as she looked into my eyes. "This event will open many doors for you. With the money we've raised, you can start your own newspaper. And many of the other ladies from Boston and Philadelphia have already expressed a wish to recreate our club in their cities. And have you speak there. With this kind of exposure, you could take your lectures to England, where there are many white people with deep pockets who are sympathetic to your crusade for justice."

She parted the curtains leading to the dais. And after one lingering look over her shoulder, she stepped into the bright stage lights.

I didn't have any background in public speaking. Sure, I

had spoken in churches and at small gatherings, urging people to buy subscriptions for my paper. But those were small, scripted instances. Not this grand magnum opus that people here were undoubtedly expecting.

In my mind, I was still a small-town girl, orphaned at a young age and scared.

But a fire simmered in my veins.

"England?" I whispered to myself.

A timid smile crossed my lips. Armed with the support of the Black New York elite, I could ride the wave of interest all the way to England. I could be like Henry "Box" Brown, who lectured in sold-out shows about his famous escape from enslavement. He smuggled himself to freedom by hiding in a box and shipping it to the North.

I lifted my chin, my chest swelling with fresh confidence. Then I stepped out onto the stage, invigorated with the urgency of my crusade for justice.

Epilogue
{ Chicago, 1923 }

I T'S BEEN DECADES SINCE THE DEATHS OF MY parents, decades since I was hugged by my father and helped my mother set the table for dinner. But if I closed my eyes, I could still taste my mother's famous home cooking, hear the laughter that filled our small but happy home. Yes, it had been a long time since I was a butterfly schoolgirl, but I still remembered everything in vivid detail.

That was my specialty. I was the one who remembered the names of the lynched, who would not forget the promises of Reconstruction. I'd made a name for myself in my fierce fight for justice. It was often lonely work. Sometimes I still got a pit of homesickness deep in my belly, and I hungered for a taste of home.

I'd tried to replicate my mother's famous cooking many times throughout the years, convinced that maybe I would somehow warm up to that domestic chore. So for what seemed like the umpteenth time, I mixed a biscuit batter, hoping for a taste of my childhood.

While my biscuits cooked, I hobbled across the hall to the living room. My heeled boots clacked against the polished wood floors of my Chicago home, which was a far cry away from the cramped quarters I rented in various Memphis boarding houses. I could scarcely believe that the house at 3624 Grand Boulevard was mine and my husband's. After so many years of toil, I had a home and a family to fill it with laughter.

The waning evening light cast shadows on the pictures that hung against the wall—pictures of my four children, pictures of my stepchildren and my husband's parents, pictures from my speaking tours of England. Sometimes I marveled at how far I'd traveled in life, given that I felt so small when I was younger. My husband and I had filled this house with family.

And it was a true partnership. We shared most household responsibilities between the two of us. To my great relief, my husband enjoyed cooking. What he put together in the kitchen on a bad day was infinitely better than what I could scrounge up. And we had hired help to pick up the slack whenever we were too busy.

We both worked full-time. At first, we were together at the *Conservator*, my husband's paper. But he moved on to become the first Black assistant state's attorney in Illinois, which afforded me the opportunity to take up the mantle of running the paper on my own and later to chair various committees. At first, I was nervous that my strong-willed nature would be off-putting to him. Not many women spoke their minds and worked so hard before marriage, let alone *after* marriage. But my husband valued my independence and free thought.

And I loved him even more for it.

Life and work continued to be as busy as it always had been. But at least this time I had a true partner to share the load. With the combination of two incomes, I had a comfortable life, and we used our resources for the good of the community. I'd never felt easy with the trappings of the Black elite, so we created a life that focused on education and activism.

This house was also where our work and our family collided.

Our home doubled as an annex to our offices. Because my husband and I both worked jobs we were passionate about, it was hard to let go of work at the end of the day. Work crept into our home, and I often found the lack of separation frustrating. Still, I couldn't help but bring work and colleagues home.

Inside the living room was my stack of newspapers from the day, which I tried to scan most every night. I was a newspaper-woman through and through. Nothing would change that—not even old age. I sat for a time, riffling through the pages of my peer publications, when my nostrils perked up.

Something smelled like it was burning.

"Oh shoot." I shot up from my chair and stomped across the hallway, blundering to a stop in front of the oven.

I looked at my wrinkly hands, hands much older than my mother's hands ever had a chance to become, and pulled out the tray of biscuits from the oven. I'd traveled a long way since my mother had baked biscuits in our family's small kitchen in Holly Springs. I'd made a name for myself in Memphis and around the country. I'd even conquered Europe *twice* with my fiery speeches condemning lynching in all its horrific forms.

But I still could not conquer cooking.

"Damn this stove." I stomped my foot, resisting the urge to kick the iron monstrosity.

"I don't think it's the stove." My husband chuckled from over my shoulder. "I think you should leave the kitchen work to me. You know my dad taught me all he knows from his time cooking on the steamboats."

"I hate cooking." I wiped my forehead with the back of my arm. I didn't know why I tried. A wife was expected to enjoy at least basic cooking, but I'd never warmed up to it. Domestic chores chaffed at my spirit, chipping away at my good mood, leaving me feeling prickly. After all these years caring for all my siblings as if they were my own children, and now with children of my own, I still did not enjoy domesticity. It frustrated the heck out of me that I couldn't conquer the kitchen like I'd conquered almost anything else I'd put my mind to. But my heart wasn't in it. In truth, I found most housework about as enjoyable as teaching. And although I felt honored to have shaped many young minds, I didn't love that vocation either. My place was at a desk with my pen or behind a lectern in front of a crowd. That was my calling.

"No need to get blue over this." My husband gently squeezed my arms. He was familiar with my bouts of depression and always tried to help me chart a course to calmer waters. "You have many talents outside the kitchen. Let me take care of these while you finish up for the day."

"I'll be in the living room." I cast my apron aside, draping it over a kitchen chair.

"Mrs. Wells-Barnett?" our maid called from the hallway. My name sounded clunky in her mouth, as if she had to work extra hard to remember to say the whole thing. Married women usually abandoned their maiden names, but I hadn't. "Will you be needing anything from the market today?"

"No, thank you." I nodded politely and stepped into the living room, eager to get back to work.

"Actually, if you could fetch more for two or three extra place settings, we do have some guests coming for dinner." My husband stepped into the hallway, smiling sheepishly as his eyes darted from the maid's to mine.

"More guests?" I raised an eyebrow. "We just entertained last week."

"I know, but as this is rather an extension of the office, I figured we could have a few more people this week to discuss a case I'm reviewing."

The maid looked between Mr. Barnett and me, her eyes darting between the two of us, who made what I was sure was the most unorthodox marriage she'd ever witnessed. I was no stranger to this shocked response. The suffragist Susan B. Anthony had also found our arrangement odd, chastising me for getting married and dividing my time between my anti-lynching calling and the domestic chores of marriage. But I found that my marriage was of a different breed.

I cleared my throat, trying to quell my rising frustration. I was guilty of bringing work home too. But I was not in the mood to open our home up again to another long dinner party.

"May I remind you that our guests last week were guests of yours," my husband said, raising his eyebrow in return, a challenge to my objections.

"I may be old, but my memory is just fine." I huffed under my breath, exasperated at having to explain my guests from the Negro Fellowship League. "I remember the people from the NFL."

"So, I'll just be off to the market then." Our maid scurried out the front door.

"She'll be buying the food as well as cooking it. Because I'm not dealing with it," I grumbled under my breath, retreating into the living room instead of making more of a fuss. It was times like this that I was incredibly thankful to have our hired help. There would be a day sometime soon when my husband or I would need to scale back on our work. With that shrinking income we wouldn't be able to afford full-time staff. But that was an issue for another day.

"Mama," my daughter called from the second-floor landing, "I'd like your opinion on some fabric."

"Well, you know that is my weakness. I always did like to dress the part, even if I hadn't arrived yet."

"I know exactly what you're going to say." Ida, my namesake, squared her shoulders. She held her head so high that her chin jutted out.

Good, I thought. I'd taught her well. A small smile tugged at my lips as I flicked my wrist at her. "I'll be up in a moment."

Then I disappeared into the study, still smiling at the young woman I'd created—a woman who held her head high.

A Black woman *should* hold her head high. She should claim her space with entitlement and without apology. There wasn't much safe space for Black people in this country, let alone a Black woman. It was up to us to make our own way, unapologetically.

My parents were at the vanguard of Reconstruction, the trailblazers of a new generation of free Black men and women. Their passion for equity and justice ran through my veins. I was a loving mother, and I would move heaven and earth for Charles, Ida, Alfreda, and Herman. I cared for my four children as much as I had cared for my younger siblings. And I hoped that I'd given my children that passion. And even though it might not be appreciated now in a time of cautious committees and organizations that didn't want to ruffle any feathers among the elite, I hoped my work in protesting lynching and racism in this country had paved the way for the next generation of activism and advocacy. That was my legacy. That was my children's legacy.

But there was still work to do.

I rolled up my sleeves and got back to it.

The following is the text that Ida B. Wells wrote and published in 1892. We feel it is important not only to know Ida's story but also read her own words.

—E. A. D. and C. B.

SOUTHERN HORRORS

LYNCH LAW

IN ALL

ITS PHASES

Miss IDA B. WELLS

THE NEW YORK AGE PRINT

1892

PREFACE

THE GREATER PART OF WHAT is contained in these pages was published in the *New York Age* June 25, 1892, in explanation of the editorial which the Memphis whites considered sufficiently infamous to justify the destruction of my paper, the *Free Speech*.

Since the appearance of that statement, requests have come from all parts of the country that "Exiled" (the name under which it then appeared) be issued in pamphlet form. Some donations were made, but not enough for that purpose. The noble effort of the ladies of New York and Brooklyn Oct. 5 have enabled me to comply with this request and give the world a true, unvarnished account of the causes of lynch law in the South.

This statement is not a shield for the despoiler of virtue, nor altogether a defense for the poor blind Afro-American Sampsons who suffer themselves to be betrayed by white Delilahs. It is a contribution to truth, an array of facts, the perusal of which it is hoped will stimulate this great American Republic to demand that justice be done though the heavens fall.

It is with no pleasure I have dipped my hands in the corruption here exposed. Somebody must show that the Afro-American race is more sinned against than sinning, and it seems to have fallen upon me to do so. The awful death-roll that Judge Lynch is calling every week is appalling, not only because of the lives it takes, the rank cruelty and outrage to the victims, but because of the prejudice it fosters and the stain it places against the good name of a weak race.

The Afro-American is not a bestial race. If this work can contribute in any way toward proving this, and at the same time arouse the conscience of the American people to a demand for justice to every citizen, and punishment by law for the lawless, I shall feel I have done my race a service. Other considerations are of minor importance.

IDA B. WELLS
New York City, Oct. 26, 1892

To the Afro-American women of New York and Brooklyn, whose race love, earnest zeal and unselfish effort at Lyric Hall, in the City of New York, on the night of October 5, 1892—made possible its publication, this pamphlet is gratefully dedicated by the author.

HON. FRED. DOUGLASS'S LETTER

Dear Miss Wells:

Let me give you thanks for your faithful paper on the lynch abomination now generally practiced against colored people in the South. There has been no word equal to it in convincing power. I have spoken, but my word is feeble in comparison. You give us what you know and testify from actual knowledge. You have dealt with the facts with cool, painstaking fidelity and left those naked and uncontradicted facts to speak for themselves.

Brave woman! You have done your people and mine a service which can neither be weighed nor measured. If American conscience were only half alive, if the American church and clergy were only half

Christianized, if American moral sensibility were not hardened by persistent infliction of outrage and crime against colored people, a scream of horror, shame and indignation would rise to Heaven wherever your pamphlet shall be read.

But alas! Even crime has power to reproduce itself and create conditions favorable to its own existence. It sometimes seems we are deserted by earth and Heaven yet we must still think, speak and work, and trust in the power of a merciful God for final deliverance.

Very truly and gratefully yours,

FREDERICK DOUGLASS

Cedar Hill, Anacostia, D.C., Oct. 25, 1892

CHAPTER I
THE OFFENSE

WEDNESDAY EVENING MAY 24, 1892, the city of Memphis was filled with excitement. Editorials in the daily papers of that date caused a meeting to be held in the Cotton Exchange Building; a committee was sent for the editors of the *Free Speech*, an Afro-American journal published in that city, and the only reason the open threats of lynching that were made were not carried out was because they could not be found. The cause of all this commotion was the following editorial published in the *Free Speech* May 21, 1892, the Saturday previous.

"Eight negroes lynched since last issue of the *Free Speech* one at Little Rock, Ark., last Saturday morning where the citizens broke(?) into the penitentiary and got their man; three near Anniston, Ala., one near New Orleans; and three at Clarksville, Ga., the last three for killing a white man, and five on the same old racket—the new alarm about raping white women. The same programme of hanging, then shooting bullets into the lifeless bodies was carried out to the letter.

Nobody in this section of the country believes the old thread-bare lie that Negro men rape white women. If Southern white men are not careful, they will overreach themselves and public sentiment will have a reaction; a conclusion will then be reached which will be very damaging to the moral reputation of their women."

The *Daily Commercial* of Wednesday following, May 25, contained the following leader:

"Those negroes who are attempting to make the lynching of individuals of their race a means for arousing the worst passions of their kind are playing with a dangerous sentiment. The negroes may as well understand that there is no mercy for the negro rapist and little patience with his defenders. A negro organ printed in this city, in a recent issue publishes the following atrocious paragraph: 'Nobody in this section of the country believes the old thread-bare lie that negro men rape white women. If Southern white men are not careful they will overreach themselves, and public sentiment will have a reaction; and a conclusion will be reached which will be very damaging to the moral reputation of their women.'

The fact that a black scoundrel is allowed to live and utter such loathsome and repulsive calumnies is a volume of evidence as to the wonderful patience of Southern whites. But we have had enough of it.

There are some things that the Southern white man will not tolerate, and the obscene intimations of the foregoing have brought the writer to the very outermost limit of public patience. We hope we have said enough."

The *Evening Scimitar* of same date, copied the *Commercial*'s editorial with these words of comment: "Patience under such circumstances is not a virtue. If the negroes themselves do not apply the remedy without delay it will be the duty of those whom he has attacked to tie the wretch who utters these calumnies to a stake at the intersection of Main and Madison Sts., brand him in the forehead with a hot iron and perform upon him a surgical operation with a pair of tailor's shears."

Acting upon this advice, the leading citizens met in the Cotton Exchange Building the same evening, and threats of lynching were freely indulged, not by the lawless element upon which the deviltry of the South is usually saddled—but by the leading business men, in their leading business centre. Mr. Fleming, the business manager and owning a half interest the *Free Speech*, had to leave town to escape the mob, and was afterwards ordered not to return; letters and telegrams sent me in New York where I was spending my vacation advised me that bodily harm awaited my return. Creditors took possession of the office and sold the outfit, and the *Free Speech* was as if it had never been.

The editorial in question was prompted by the many inhuman and fiendish lynchings of Afro-Americans which have recently taken place and was meant as a warning. Eight lynched in one week and five of them charged with rape! The thinking public will not easily believe freedom and education more brutalizing than slavery, and the world knows that the crime of rape was unknown during four years of civil war, when the white women of the South were at the mercy of the race which is all at once charged with being a bestial one.

Since my business has been destroyed and I am an exile from home because of that editorial, the issue has been forced, and as the writer of it I feel that the race and the public generally should have a statement of the facts as they exist. They will serve at the same time as a defense for the Afro-Americans Sampsons who suffer themselves to be betrayed by white Delilahs.

The whites of Montgomery, Ala., knew J.C. Duke sounded the keynote of the situation—which they would gladly hide from the world, when he said in his paper, the *Herald*, five years ago: "Why is it that white women attract negro men now more than in former days? There was a time when such a thing was unheard of. There is a secret to this thing, and we greatly suspect it is the growing appreciation of white Juliets for colored Romeos." Mr. Duke, like the *Free Speech* proprietors, was forced to leave the city for reflecting on the "honah" of white women and his paper suppressed; but the truth remains that Afro-American men do not always rape(?) white women without their consent.

Mr. Duke, before leaving Montgomery, signed a card disclaiming any intention of slandering Southern white women. The editor of the *Free Speech* has no disclaimer to enter, but asserts instead that there are many white women in the South who would marry colored men if such an act would not place them at once beyond the pale of society and within the clutches of the law. The miscegenation laws of the South only operate against the legitimate union of the races; they leave the white man free to seduce all the colored girls he can, but it is death to the colored man who yields to the force and advances of a similar attraction in white women. White men lynch the offending Afro-American, not because he is a despoiler of virtue, but because he succumbs to the smiles of white women.

CHAPTER II
THE BLACK AND WHITE OF IT

THE *CLEVELAND GAZETTE* OF January 16, 1892, publishes a case in point. Mrs. J. S. Underwood, the wife of a minister of Elyria, Ohio, accused an Afro-American of rape. She told her husband that during his absence in 1888, stumping the State for the Prohibition Party, the man came to the kitchen door, forced his way in the house and insulted her. She tried to drive him out with a heavy poker, but he overpowered and chloroformed her, and when she revived her clothing was torn and she was in a horrible condition. She did not know the man but could identify him. She pointed out William Offett, a married man, who was arrested and, being in Ohio, was granted a trial.

The prisoner vehemently denied the charge of rape, but confessed he went to Mrs. Underwood's residence at her invitation and was criminally intimate with her at her request. This availed him nothing against the sworn testimony of a ministers wife, a lady of the highest respectability. He was found guilty, and entered the penitentiary, December 14, 1888, for fifteen years. Some time afterwards the woman's remorse led her to confess to her husband that the man was innocent.

These are her words: "I met Offett at the Post Office. It was raining. He was polite to me, and as I had several bundles in my arms he offered to carry them home for me, which he did. He had a strange fascination for me, and I invited him to call on me. He called, bringing chestnuts and candy for the children. By this means we got them to leave us alone in the room. Then I sat on his lap. He made a proposal to me and I readily consented. Why I did so, I do not know, but that I did is true. He visited me several times after that and each time I was indiscreet. I did not care after the first time. In fact I could not have resisted, and had no desire to resist."

When asked by her husband why she told him she had been outraged, she said: "I had several reasons for telling you. One was the neighbors saw the fellows here, another was, I was afraid I had contracted a loathsome disease, and still another was that I feared I might give birth to a Negro baby. I hoped to save my reputation by telling you a deliberate lie." Her husband horrified by the confession had Offett, who had already served four years, released and secured a divorce.

There are thousands of such cases throughout the South, with the difference that the Southern white men in insatiate fury wreak their vengeance without intervention of law upon the Afro-Americans who consort with their women. A few instances to substantiate the assertion that some white women love the company of the Afro-American will not be out of place. Most of these cases were reported by the daily papers of the South.

In the winter of 1885–86 the wife of a practicing physician in Memphis, in good social standing whose name has escaped me, left home, husband and children, and ran away with her black coachman. She was with him a month before her husband found and brought her home. The coachman could not be found. The doctor moved his family away from Memphis, and is living in another city under an assumed name.

In the same city last year a white girl in the dusk of

evening screamed at the approach of some parties that a Negro had assaulted her on the street. He was captured, tried by a white judge and jury, that acquitted him of the charge. It is needless to add if there had been a scrap of evidence on which to convict him of so grave a charge he would have been convicted.

Sarah Clark of Memphis loved a black man and lived openly with him. When she was indicted last spring for miscegenation, she swore in court that she was *not* a white woman. This she did to escape the penitentiary and continued her illicit relation undisturbed. That she is of the lower class of whites, does not disturb the fact that she is a white woman. "The leading citizens" of Memphis are defending the "honor" of *all* white women, *demi-monde* included.

Since the manager of the *Free Speech* has been run away from Memphis by the guardians of the honor of Southern white women, a young girl living on Poplar St., who was discovered in intimate relations with a handsome mulatto young colored man, Will Morgan by name, stole her father's money to send the young fellow away from that father's wrath. She has since joined him in Chicago.

The *Memphis Ledger* for June 8 has the following: "If Lillie Bailey, a rather pretty white girl seventeen years of age, who is now at the City Hospital, would be somewhat less reserved about her disgrace there would be some very nauseating details in the story of her life. She is the mother of a little coon. The truth might reveal fearful depravity or it might reveal the evidence of a rank outrage. She will not divulge the name of the man who has left such black evidence of her disgrace, and, in fact, says it is a matter in which there can be no interest to the outside world. She came to Memphis nearly three months ago and was taken in at the Woman's Refuge in the southern part of the city. She remained there until a few weeks ago, when the child was born. The ladies in charge of the Refuge were horrified. The girl was at once sent to the City Hospital, where she has been since May 30. She is a country girl. She came to Memphis from her father's farm, a short distance from Hernando, Miss. Just when she left there she would not say. In fact she says she came to Memphis from Arkansas, and says her home is in that State. She is rather good looking, has blue eyes, a low forehead and dark red hair. The ladies at the Woman's Refuge do not know anything about the girl further than what they learned when she was an inmate of the institution; and she would not tell much. When the child was born an attempt was made to get the girl to reveal the name of the Negro who had disgraced her, she obstinately refused and it was impossible to elicit any information from her on the subject."

Note the wording. "The truth might reveal fearful depravity or rank outrage." If it had been a white child or Lillie Bailey had told a pitiful story of Negro outrage, it would have been a case of woman's weakness or assault and she could have remained at the Woman's Refuge. But a Negro child and to withhold its father's name and thus prevent the killing of another Negro "rapist." A case of "fearful depravity."

The very week the "leading citizens" of Memphis were making a spectacle of themselves in defense of all white women of every kind, an Afro-American, M. Stricklin, was found in a white woman's room in that city. Although she made no outcry of rape, he was jailed and would have been lynched, but the woman stated she bought curtains of him (he was a furniture dealer) and his business in her room that night was to put them up. A white woman's word was taken as absolutely in this case as when the cry of rape is made, and he was freed.

What is true of Memphis is true of the entire South. The daily papers last year reported a farmer's wife in Alabama had given birth to a Negro child. When the Negro farm hand who was plowing in the field heard it he took the mule from the plow and fled. The dispatches also told of a woman in South Carolina who gave birth to a Negro child and charged three men with being its father, *every one of whom has since disappeared*. In Tuscumbia, Ala., the colored boy who was lynched there last year for assaulting a white girl told her before his accusers that he had met her there in the woods often before.

Frank Weems of Chattanooga who was not lynched in May only because the prominent citizens became his body guard until the doors of the penitentiary closed on him, had letters in his pocket from the white woman in the case, making the appointment with him. Edward Coy who was burned alive in Texarkana, January 1, 1892, died protesting his innocence. Investigation since as given by the Bystander in the *Chicago Inter-Ocean*, October 1, proves:

"1. The woman who was paraded as a victim of violence was of bad character; her husband was a drunkard and a gambler.

2. She was publicly reported and generally known to have been criminally intimate with Coy for more than a year previous.

3. She was compelled by threats, if not by violence, to make the charge against the victim.

4. When she came to apply the match Coy asked her if she would burn him after they had 'been sweet-hearting' so long.

5. A large majority of the 'superior' white men prominent in the affair are the reputed fathers of mulatto children.

These are not pleasant facts, but they are illustrative of the vital phase of the so-called 'race question,' which should properly be designated an earnest inquiry as to the best methods by which religion, science, law and political power may be employed to excuse injustice, barbarity and crime done to a people because of race and color. There can be no possible belief that these people were inspired by any consuming zeal to vindicate God's law against miscegenationists of the most practical sort. The woman was a willing partner in the victim's guilt, and being of the 'superior' race must naturally have been more guilty."

In Natchez, Miss., Mrs. Marshall, one of the *creme de la creme* of the city, created a tremendous sensation several years ago. She has a black coachman who was married, and had been in her employ several years. During this time she gave birth to a child whose color was remarked, but traced to some brunette ancestor, and one of the fashionable dames of the city was its godmother. Mrs. Marshall's social position was unquestioned, and wealth showered every dainty on this child which was idolized with its brothers and sisters by its white papa. In course of time another child appeared on the scene, but it was unmistakably dark. All were alarmed, and "rush of blood, strangulation" were the conjectures, but the doctor, when asked the cause, grimly told them it was a Negro child. There was a family conclave, the coachman heard of it and leaving his own family went West, and has never returned. As soon as Mrs. Marshall was able to travel she was sent away in deep disgrace. Her husband died within the year of a broken heart.

Ebenzer Fowler, the wealthiest colored man in Issaquena County, Miss., was shot down on the street in Mayersville, January 30, 1885, just before dark by an armed body of white men who filled his body with bullets. They charged him with writing a note to a white woman of the place, which they intercepted and which proved there was an intimacy existing between them.

Hundreds of such cases might be cited, but enough have been given to prove the assertion that there are white women in the South who love the Afro-American's company even as there are white men notorious for their preference for Afro-American women.

There is hardly a town in the South which has not an instance of the kind which is well known, and hence the assertion is reiterated that "nobody in the South believes the old thread bare lie that negro men rape white women." Hence there is a growing demand among Afro-Americans that the guilt or innocence of parties accused of rape be fully established. They know the men of the section of the country who refuse this are not so desirous of punishing rapists as they pretend. The utterances of the leading white men show that with them it is not the crime but the *class*. Bishop Fitzgerald has become apologist for lynchers of the rapists of *white* women only. Governor Tillman, of South Carolina, in the month of June, standing under the tree in Barnwell, S.C., on which eight Afro-Americans were hung last year, declared that he would lead a mob to lynch a *negro* who raped a *white* woman. So say the pulpits, officials and newspapers of the South. But when the victim is a colored woman it is different.

Last winter in Baltimore, Md., three white ruffians assaulted a Miss Camphor, a young Afro-American girl, while out walking with a young man of her own race. They held her escort and outraged the girl. It was a deed dastardly enough to arouse Southern blood, which gives its horror of rape as excuse for lawlessness, but she was an Afro-American. The case went to the courts, an Afro-American lawyer defended the men and they were acquitted.

In Nashville, Tenn., there is a white man, Pat Hanifan, who outraged a little Afro-American girl, and, from the physical injuries received, she has been ruined for life. He was jailed for six months, discharged, and is now a detective in that city. In the same city, last May, a white man outraged an Afro-American girl in a drug store. He was arrested, and released on bail at the trial. It was rumored that five hundred Afro-Americans had organized to lynch him. Two hundred and fifty white citizens armed themselves with Winchesters and guarded him. A cannon was placed in front of his home, and the Buchanan Rifles (State Militia) ordered to the scene for his protection. The Afro-American mob did not materialize. Only two weeks before Eph. Grizzard, who had only been *charged* with rape upon a white woman, had been taken from the jail, with Governor Buchanan and the police and militia standing by, dragged through the streets in broad daylight, knives plunged into him at every step, and with every fiendish cruelty a frenzied mob could devise, he was at last swung out on the bridge with hands cut to pieces as he tried to climb up the stanchions. A naked, bloody example of the blood-thirstiness of the nineteenth-century civilization of the Athens of the South! No cannon or military was called out in his defense. He dared to visit a white woman.

At the very moment these civilized whites were announcing their determination "to protect their wives and daughters," by murdering Grizzard, a white man was in the same jail for raping eight-year-old Maggie Reese, an Afro-American girl. He was not harmed. The "honor" of grown women who were glad enough to be supported by the Grizzard boys and Ed Coy, as long as the liaison was not known, needed protection; they were white. The outrage upon helpless childhood needed no avenging in this case; she was black.

A white man in Guthrie, Oklahoma Territory, two months ago inflicted such injuries upon another Afro-American child that she died. He was not punished, but an attempt was made in the same town in the month of June to lynch an Afro-American who visited a white woman.

In Memphis, Tenn., in the month of June, Ellerton L. Dorr, who is the husband of Russell Hancock's widow, was arrested for attempted rape on Mattie Cole, a neighbors cook; he was only prevented from accomplishing his purpose, by the appearance of Mattie's employer. Dorr's friends say he was drunk and not responsible for his actions. The grand jury refused to indict him and he was discharged.

CHAPTER III
THE NEW CRY

THE APPEAL OF SOUTHERN WHITES to Northern sympathy and sanction, the adroit, insidious plea made by Bishop Fitzgerald for suspension of judgment because those "who condemn lynching express no sympathy for the *white* woman in the case," falls to the ground in the light of the foregoing.

From this exposition of the race issue in lynch law, the whole matter is explained by the well-known opposition growing out of slavery to the progress of the race. This is crystalized in the oft-repeated slogan: "This is a white man's country and the white man must rule." The South resented giving the Afro-American his freedom, the ballot box and the Civil Rights Law. The raids of the Ku-Klux and White Liners to subvert reconstruction government, the Hamburg and Ellenton, S.C., the Copiah County, Miss., and the Lafayette Parish, La., massacres were excused as the natural resentment of intelligence against government by ignorance.

Honest white men practically conceded the necessity of intelligence murdering ignorance to correct the mistake of the general government, and the race was left to the tender mercies of the solid South. Thoughtful Afro-Americans with the strong arm of the government withdrawn and with the hope to stop such wholesale massacres urged the race to sacrifice its political rights for sake of peace. They honestly believed the race should fit itself for government, and when that should be done, the objection to race participation in politics would be removed.

But the sacrifice did not remove the trouble, nor move the South to justice. One by one the Southern States have legally(?) disfranchised the Afro-American, and since the repeal of the Civil Rights Bill nearly every Southern State has passed separate car laws with a penalty against their infringement. The race regardless of advancement is penned into filthy, stifling partitions cut off from smoking cars. All this while, although the political cause has been removed, the butcheries of black men at Barnwell, S.C., Carrolton, Miss., Waycross, Ga., and Memphis, Tenn., have gone on; also the flaying alive of a man in Kentucky, the burning of one in Arkansas, the hanging of a fifteen-year-old girl in Louisiana, a woman in Jackson, Tenn., and one in Hollendale, Miss., until the dark and bloody record of the South shows 728 Afro-Americans lynched during the past eight years. Not fifty of these were for political causes; the rest were for all manner of accusations from that of rape of white women, to the case of the boy Will Lewis who was hanged at Tullahoma, Tenn., last year for being drunk and "sassy" to white folks.

These statistics compiled by the *Chicago Tribune* were given the first of this year (1892). Since then, not less than one hundred and fifty have been known to have met violent death at the hands of cruel bloodthirsty mobs during the past nine months.

To palliate this record (which grows worse as the Afro-American becomes intelligent) and excuse some of the most heinous crimes that ever stained the history of a country, the South is shielding itself behind the plausible screen of defending the honor of its women. This, too, in the face of the fact that only *one-third* of the 728 victims to mobs have been *charged* with rape, to say nothing of those of that one-third who were innocent of the charge. A white correspondent of the *Baltimore Sun* declares that the Afro-American who was lynched in Chestertown, Md., in May for assault on a white girl was innocent; that the deed was done by a white man who had since disappeared. The girl herself maintained that her assailant was a white man. When that poor Afro-American was murdered, the whites excused their refusal of a trial on the ground that they wished to spare the white girl the mortification of having to testify in court.

This cry has had its effect. It has closed the heart, stifled the conscience, warped the judgment and hushed the voice of press and pulpit on the subject of lynch law throughout this "land of liberty." Men who stand high in the esteem of the public for Christian character, for moral and physical courage, for devotion to the principles of equal and exact justice to all, and for great sagacity, stand as cowards who fear to open their mouths before this great outrage. They do not see that by their tacit encouragement, their silent acquiescence, the black shadow of lawlessness in the form of lynch law is spreading its wings over the whole country.

Men who, like Governor Tillman, start the ball

of lynch law rolling for a certain crime, are powerless to stop it when drunken or criminal white toughs feel like hanging an Afro-American on any pretext.

Even to the better class of Afro-Americans the crime of rape is so revolting they have too often taken the white man's word and given lynch law neither the investigation nor condemnation it deserved.

They forget that a concession of the right to lynch a man for a certain crime, not only concedes the right to lynch any person for any crime, but (so frequently is the cry of rape now raised) it is in a fair way to stamp us a race of rapists and desperadoes. They have gone on hoping and believing that general education and financial strength would solve the difficulty, and are devoting their energies to the accumulation of both.

The mob spirit has grown with the increasing intelligence of the Afro-American. It has left the out-of-the-way places where ignorance prevails, has thrown off the mask and with this new cry stalks in broad daylight in large cities, the centers of civilization, and is encouraged by the "leading citizens" and the press.

CHAPTER IV
THE MALICIOUS AND UNTRUTHFUL WHITE PRESS

THE *DAILY COMMERCIAL* AND *Evening Scimitar* of Memphis, Tenn., are owned by leading business men of that city, and yet, in spite of the fact that there had been no white woman in Memphis outraged by an Afro-American, and that Memphis possessed a thrifty law-abiding, property-owning class of Afro-Americans the *Commercial* of May 17, under the head of "More Rapes, More Lynchings" gave utterance to the following:

The lynching of three Negro scoundrels reported in our dispatches from Anniston, Ala., for a brutal outrage committed upon a white woman will be a text for much comment on "Southern barbarism" by Northern newspapers; but we fancy it will hardly prove effective for campaign purposes among intelligent people. The frequency of these lynchings calls attention to the frequency of the crimes which causes lynching. The "Southern barbarism" which deserves the serious attention of all people North and South, is the barbarism which preys upon weak and defenseless women. Nothing but the most prompt, speedy and extreme punishment can hold in check the horrible and bestial propensities of the Negro race. There is a strange similarity about a number of cases of this character which have lately occurred.

In each case the crime was deliberately planned and perpetrated by several Negroes. They watched for an opportunity when the women were left without a protector. It was not a sudden yielding to a fit of passion, but the consummation of a devilish purpose which has been seeking and waiting for the opportunity. This feature of the crime not only makes it the most fiendishly brutal, but it adds to the terror of the situation in the thinly settled country communities. No man can leave his family at night without the dread that some roving Negro ruffian is watching and waiting for this opportunity. The swift punishment which invariably follows these horrible crimes doubtless acts as a deterring effect upon the Negroes in that immediate neighborhood for a short time. But the lesson is not widely learned nor long remembered. Then such crimes, equally atrocious, have happened in quick succession, one in Tennessee, one in Arkansas, and one in Alabama. The facts of the crime appear to appeal more to the Negro's lustful imagination than the facts of the punishment do to his fears. He sets aside all fear of death in any form when opportunity is found for the gratification of his bestial desires.

There is small reason to hope for any change for the better. The commission of this crime grows more frequent every year. The generation of Negroes which have grown up since the war have lost in large measure the traditional and wholesome awe of the white race which kept the Negroes in subjection, even when their masters were in the army, and their families left unprotected except by the slaves themselves. There is no longer a restraint upon the brute passion of the Negro.

What is to be done? The crime of rape is always horrible, but the Southern man there is nothing which so fills the soul with horror, loathing and fury as the outraging of a white woman by a Negro. It is the race question in the ugliest, vilest, most dangerous aspect. The Negro as a political factor can be controlled. But neither laws nor lynchings can subdue his lusts. Sooner or later it will force a crisis. We do not know in what form it will come."

In its issue of June 4, the *Memphis Evening Scimitar* gives the following excuse for lynch law:

"Aside from the violation of white women by Negroes, which is the outcropping of a bestial perversion of instinct, the chief cause of trouble between the races in the South is the Negro's lack of manners. In the state of slavery he learned politeness from association with white people, who took pains to teach him. Since the emancipation came and the tie of mutual interest and regard between master and servant was broken, the Negro has drifted away into a state which is neither freedom nor bondage. Lacking the proper inspiration of the one and the restraining force of the other he has taken up the idea that boorish insolence is independence, and the exercise of a decent degree of breeding toward white people is identical with servile submission. In consequence of the prevalence of this notion there are many Negroes who use every opportunity to make themselves offensive, particularly when they think it can be done with impunity.

We have had too many instances right here in Memphis to doubt this, and our experience is not exceptional. *The white people won't stand this sort of thing, and whether they be insulted as individuals are as a race, the response will be prompt and effectual.* The bloody riot of 1866, in which so many Negroes perished, was brought on principally by the outrageous conduct of the blacks toward the whites on the streets. It is also a remarkable and discouraging fact that the majority of such scoundrels are Negroes who have received educational advantages at the hands of the white taxpayers. They have got just enough of learning to make them realize how hopelessly their race is behind the other in everything that makes a great people, and they attempt to "get even" by insolence, which is ever the resentment of inferiors. There are well-bred Negroes among us, and it is truly unfortunate that they should have to pay, even in part, the penalty of the offenses committed by the baser sort, but this is the way of the world. The innocent must suffer for the guilty. If the Negroes as a people possessed a hundredth part of the self-respect which is evidenced by the courteous bearing of some that the *Scimitar* could name, the friction between the races would be reduced to a minimum. It will not do to beg the question by pleading that many white men are also stirring up strife. The Caucasian blackguard simply obeys the promptings of a depraved disposition, and he is seldom deliberately rough or offensive toward strangers or unprotected women.

The Negro tough, on the contrary, is given to just that kind of offending, and he almost invariably singles out white people as his victims.

On March 9, 1892, there were lynched in this same city three of the best specimens of young since-the-war Afro-American manhood. They were peaceful, law-abiding citizens and energetic business men.

They believed the problem was to be solved by eschewing politics and putting money in the purse. They owned a flourishing grocery business in a thickly populated suburb of Memphis, and a white man named Barrett had one on the opposite corner. After a personal difficulty which Barrett sought by going into the "People's Grocery" drawing a pistol and was thrashed by Calvin McDowell, he (Barrett) threatened to "clean them out." These men were a mile beyond the city limits and police protection; hearing that Barrett's crowd was coming to attack them Saturday night, they mustered forces, and prepared to defend themselves against the attack.

When Barrett came he led a *posse* of officers, twelve in number, who afterward claimed to be hunting a man for whom they had a warrant. That twelve men in citizen's clothes should think it necessary to go in the night to hunt one man who had never before been arrested, or made any record as a criminal has never been explained. When they entered the back door the young men thought the threatened attack was on, and fired into them. Three of the officers were wounded, and when the *defending* party found it was officers of the law upon whom they had fired, they ceased and got away.

Thirty-one men were arrested and thrown in jail as "conspirators," although they all declared more than once they did not know they were firing on officers. Excitement was at fever beat until the morning papers, two days after, announced that the wounded deputy sheriffs were out of danger. This hindered rather than helped the plans of the whites. There was no law on the statute books which would execute an Afro-American for wounding a white man, but the "unwritten law" did. Three of these men, the president, the manager and clerk of the grocery—"the leaders of the conspiracy"—were secretly taken from jail and lynched in a shockingly brutal manner. "The Negroes are getting too independent," they say, "we must teach them a lesson."

What lesson? The lesson of subordination. "Kill

the leaders and it will cow the Negro who dares to shoot a white man, even in self-defense."

Although the race was wild over the outrage, the mockery of law and justice which disarmed men and locked them up in jails where they could be easily and safely reached by the mob—the Afro-American ministers, newspapers and leaders counselled obedience to the law which did not protect them.

Their counsel was heeded and not a hand was uplifted to resent the outrage; following the advice of the *Free Speech*, people left the city in great numbers.

The dailies and associated press reports heralded these men to the country as "toughs," and "Negro desperadoes who kept a low dive." This same press service printed that the Negro who was lynched at Indianola, Miss., in May, had outraged the sheriff's eight-year-old daughter. The girl was more than eighteen years old, and was found by her father in this man's room, who was a servant on the place.

Not content with misrepresenting the race, the mob-spirit was not to be satisfied until the paper which was doing all it could to counteract this impression was silenced. The colored people were resenting their bad treatment in a way to make itself felt, yet gave the mob no excuse for further murder, until the appearance of the editorial which is construed as a reflection on the "honor" of the Southern white women. It is not half so libelous as that of the *Commercial* which appeared four days before, and which has been given in these pages. They would have lynched the manager of the *Free Speech* for exercising the right of free speech if they had found him as quickly as they would have hung a rapist, and glad of the excuse to do so. The owners were ordered not to return, the *Free Speech* was suspended with as little compunction as the business of the "People's Grocery" broken up and the proprietors murdered.

CHAPTER V
THE SOUTH'S POSITION

ENRY W. GRADY IN HIS WELL-remembered speeches in New England and New York pictured the Afro-American as incapable of self-government. Through him and other leading men the cry of the South to the country has been "Hands off! Leave us to solve our problem." To the Afro-American the South says, "the white man must and will rule." There is little difference between the Antebellum South and the New South.

Her white citizens are wedded to any method however revolting, any measure however extreme, for the subjugation of the young manhood of the race. They have cheated him out of his ballot, deprived him of civil rights or redress therefor in the civil courts, robbed him of the fruits of his labor, and are still murdering, burning and lynching him.

The result is a growing disregard of human life. Lynch law has spread its insidious influence till men in New York State, Pennsylvania and on the free Western plains feel they can take the law in their own hands with impunity, especially where an Afro-American is concerned. The South is brutalized to a degree not realized by its own inhabitants, and the very foundation of government, law and order, are imperiled.

Public sentiment has had a slight "reaction" though not sufficient to stop the crusade of lawlessness and lynching. The spirit of Christianity of the great M. E. Church was aroused to the frequent and revolting crimes against a weak people, enough to pass strong condemnatory resolutions at its General Conference in Omaha last May. The spirit of justice of the grand old party asserted itself sufficiently to secure a denunciation of the wrongs, and a feeble declaration of the belief in human rights in the Republican platform at Minneapolis, June 7. Some of the great dailies and weeklies have swung into line declaring that lynch law must go. The President of the United States issued a proclamation that it be not tolerated in the territories over which he has jurisdiction. Governor Northern and Chief Justice Bleckley of Georgia have proclaimed against it. The citizens of Chattanooga, Tenn., have set a worthy example in that they not only condemn lynch law, but her public men demanded a trial for Weems, the accused rapist, and guarded him while the trial was in progress. The trial only lasted ten minutes, and Weems chose to plead guilty and accept twenty-one years sentence, than invite the certain death which awaited him outside that cordon of police if he had told the truth and shown the letters he had from the white woman in the case.

Col. A. S. Colyar, of Nashville, Tenn., is so overcome with the horrible state of affairs that he addressed the following earnest letter to the *Nashville American.* "Nothing since I have been a reading man has so impressed me with the decay of manhood among the people of Tennessee as the dastardly submission to the mob reign. We have reached the unprecedented low level; the awful criminal depravity of substituting the mob for the court and jury, of giving up the jail keys to the mob whenever they are demanded. We do it in the largest cities and in the country towns; we do it in midday; we do it after full, not to say formal, notice, and so thoroughly and generally is it acquiesced in that the murderers have discarded the formula of masks. They go into the town where everybody knows them, sometimes under the gaze of the governor, in the presence of the courts, in the presence of the sheriff and his deputies, in the presence of the entire police force, take out the prisoner, take his life, often with fiendish glee, and often with acts of cruelty and barbarism which impress the reader with a degeneracy rapidly approaching savage life. That the State is disgraced but faintly expresses the humiliation which has settled upon the once proud people of Tennessee. The State, in its majesty, through its organized life, for which the people pay liberally, makes but one record, but one note, and that a criminal falsehood, 'was hung by persons to the jury unknown.' The murder at Shelbyville is only a verification of what every intelligent man knew would come, because with a mob a rumor is as good as a proof."

These efforts brought forth apologies and a short halt, but the lynching mania was raged again through the past three months with unabated fury.

The strong arm of the law must be brought to bear upon lynchers in severe punishment, but this cannot and will not be done unless a healthy public sentiment demands and sustains such action.

The men and women in the South who disapprove

of lynching and remain silent on the perpetration of such outrages, are *particeps criminis*, accomplices, accessories before and after the fact, equally guilty with the actual lawbreakers who would not persist if they did not know that neither the law nor militia would be employed against them.

CHAPTER VI
SELF-HELP

IN THE CREATION OF THIS HEALTH-ier public sentiment, the Afro-American can do for himself what no one else can do for him. The world looks on with wonder that we have conceded so much and remain law-abiding under such great outrage and provocation.

To Northern capital and Afro-American labor the South owes its rehabilitation. If labor is withdrawn capital will not remain. The Afro-American is thus the backbone of the South. A thorough knowledge and judicious exercise of this power in lynching localities could many times effect a bloodless revolution. The white man's dollar is his god, and to stop this will be to stop outrages in many localities.

The Afro-Americans of Memphis denounced the lynching of three of their best citizens, and urged and waited for the authorities to act in the matter and bring the lynchers to justice. No attempt was made to do so, and the black men left the city by thousands, bringing about great stagnation in every branch of business. Those who remained so injured the business of the street car company by staying off the cars, that the superintendent, manager and treasurer called personally on the editor of the *Free Speech*, asked them to urge our people to give them their patronage again. Other business men became alarmed over the situation and the *Free Speech* was run away that the colored people might be more easily controlled. A meeting of white citizens in June, three months after the lynching, passed resolutions for the first time, condemning it. *But they did not punish the lynchers.* Every one of them was known by name, because they had been selected to do the dirty work, by some of the very citizens who passed these resolutions. Memphis is fast losing her black population, who proclaim as they go that there is no protection for the life and property of any Afro-American citizen in Memphis who is not a slave.

The Afro-American citizens of Kentucky, whose

intellectual and financial improvement has been phenomenal, have never had a separate car law until now. Delegations and petitions poured into the Legislature against it, yet the bill passed and the Jim Crow Car of Kentucky is a legalized institution. Will the great mass of Negroes continue to patronize the railroad? A special from Covington, Ky., says:

Covington, June 13.—The railroads of the State are beginning to feel very markedly, the effects of the separate coach bill recently passed by the Legislature. No class of people in the State have so many and so largely attended excursions as the blacks. All these have been abandoned, and regular travel is reduced to a minimum. A competent authority says the loss to the various roads will reach $1,000,000 this year.

A call to a State Conference in Lexington, Ky., last June had delegates from every county in the State. Those delegates, the ministers, teachers, heads of secret and other orders, and the head of every family should pass the word around for every member of the race in Kentucky to stay off railroads unless obliged to ride. If they did so, and their advice was followed persistently the convention would not need to petition the Legislature to repeal the law or raise money to file a suit. The railroad corporations would be so effected they would in self-defense lobby to have the separate car law repealed. On the other hand, as long as the railroads can get Afro-American excursions they will always have plenty of money to fight all the suits brought against them. They will be aided in so doing by the same partisan public sentiment which passed the law. White men passed the law, and white judges and juries would pass upon the suits against the law, and render judgment in line with their prejudices and in deference to the greater financial power.

The appeal to the white man's pocket has ever been more effectual than all the appeals ever made to his conscience. Nothing, absolutely nothing, is to be gained by a further sacrifice of manhood and self-respect. By the right exercise of his power as the industrial factor of the South, the Afro-American can demand and secure his rights, the punishment of lynchers, and a fair trial for accused rapists.

Of the many inhuman outrages of this present year, the only case where the proposed lynching did *not* occur, was where the men armed themselves in Jacksonville, Fla., and Paducah, Ky, and prevented it. The only times an Afro-American who was assaulted got away has been when he had a gun and used it in self-defense.

The lesson this teaches and which every Afro-American should ponder well, is that a Winchester rifle should have a place of honor in every black home, and it should be used for that protection which the law refuses to give. When the white man who is always the aggressor knows he runs as great risk of biting the dust every time his Afro-American victim does, he will have greater respect for Afro-American life. The more the Afro-American yields and cringes and begs, the more he has to do so, the more he is insulted, outraged and lynched.

The assertion has been substantiated throughout these pages that the press contains unreliable and doctored reports of lynchings, and one of the most necessary things for the race to do is to get these facts before the public. The people must know before they can act, and there is no educator to compare with the press.

The Afro-American papers are the only ones which will print the truth, and they lack means to employ agents and detectives to get at the facts. The race must rally a mighty host to the support of their journals, and thus enable them to do much in the way of investigation.

A lynching occurred at Port Jarvis, N.Y., the first week in June. A white and colored man were implicated in the assault upon a white girl. It was charged that the white man paid the colored boy to make the assault, which he did on the public highway in broad day time, and was lynched. This, too was done by "parties unknown." The white man in the case still lives. He was imprisoned and promises to fight the case on trial. At the preliminary examination, it developed that he had been a suitor of the girl's. She had repulsed and refused him, yet had given him money, and he had sent threatening letters demanding more.

The day before this examination she was so wrought up, she left home and wandered miles away. When found she said she did so because she was afraid of the man's testimony. Why should she be afraid of the prisoner! Why should she yield to his demands for money if not to prevent him exposing something he knew! It seems explainable only on the hypothesis that a *liaison* existed between the colored boy and the girl, and the white man knew of it. The press is singularly silent. Has it a motive? We owe it to ourselves to find out.

The story comes from Larned, Kansas, Oct. 1, that a young white lady held at bay until daylight, without alarming any one in the house, "a burly Negro" who entered her room and bed. The "burly Negro" was promptly lynched without investigation or examination of inconsistent stories.

A house was found burned down near Montgomery, Ala., in Monroe County, Oct. 13, a few weeks ago; also the burned bodies of the owners and melted piles of gold and silver.

These discoveries led to the conclusion that the awful crime was not prompted by motives of robbery. The suggestion of the whites was that "brutal lust was the incentive, and as there are nearly 200 Negroes living within a radius of five miles of the place the conclusion was inevitable that some of them were the perpetrators."

Upon this "suggestion" probably made by the real criminal, the mob acted upon the "conclusion" and arrested ten Afro-Americans, four of whom, they tell the world, confessed to the deed of murdering Richard L. Johnson and outraging his daughter, Jeanette. These four men, Berrell Jones, Moses Johnson, Jim and John Packer, none of them twenty-five years of age, upon this conclusion, were taken from jail, hanged, shot, and burned while yet alive the night of Oct. 12. The same report says Mr. Johnson was on the best of terms with his Negro tenants.

The race thus outraged must find out the facts of

this awful hurling of men into eternity on supposition, and give them to the indifferent and apathetic country. We feel this to be a garbled report, but how can we prove it?

Near Vicksburg, Miss., a murder was committed by a gang of burglars. Of course it must have been done by Negroes, and Negroes were arrested for it. It is believed that two men, Smith Tooley and John Adams belonged to a gang controlled by white men and, fearing exposure, on the night of July 4, they were hanged in the Court House yard by those interested in silencing them. Robberies since committed in the same vicinity have been known to be by white men who had their faces blackened. We strongly believe in the innocence of these murdered men, but we have no proof. No other news goes out to the world save that which stamps us as a race of cutthroats, robbers and lustful wild beasts. So great is Southern hate and prejudice, they legally(?) hung poor little thirteen-year-old Mildrey Brown at Columbia, S.C., Oct. 7, on the circumstantial evidence that she poisoned a white infant. If her guilt had been proven unmistakably, had she been white, Mildrey Brown would never have been hung.

The country would have been aroused and South

Carolina disgraced forever for such a crime. The Afro-American himself did not know as he should have known as his journals should be in a position to have him know and act.

Nothing is more definitely settled than he must act for himself. I have shown how he may employ the boycott, emigration and the press, and I feel that by a combination of all these agencies can be effectually stamped out lynch law, that last relic of barbarism and slavery. "The gods help those who help themselves."